The Girl Most Likely

a Class of '85 Reunion story

by

Jana Richards

The Girl Most Likely: Class of '85 Reunion Series

The Wild Rose Press
PO Box 708
Adams Basin, NY 14410-0706
Visit us at www.thewildrosepress.com

Publishing History
First *Last Rose of Summer* Edition, 2011
Print ISBN 978-1-5092-0453-3
Digital ISBN 978-1-61217-182-1

Published in the United States of America

He chuckled. "Jessica better watch her back. You could give her a run for her money."

Cara's throaty laugh made various parts of his anatomy tingle in response. "Yes, that's my evil plan. Take over *Rochester Noon*, then the world."

"If you set your mind to it, I'm sure you could do it."

"Thanks, Finn."

"For what?"

"Believing in me."

"Are you going to be okay now?"

"I'm fine. Thanks to you."

He wanted so badly to tell her he loved her, adored her, thought she was the most amazing woman in the world. Fear stopped him. Was she truly over her ex-husband? Why else would losing weight for the reunion be so important to her if not to impress Peter?

"I've got to run," she said. "Thanks again. I'll talk to you later at my condo, right?"

"Absolutely. I can hardly wait to hear about your big TV debut. Break a leg. Isn't that what they say in show biz?"

She laughed. "Yeah, that's what they say. Bye."

Finn replaced the receiver and closed his eyes. *Why doesn't she realize how amazing she is?*

Then again, if she did would there still be room in her life for him?

What People Are Saying
about Jana Richards...

FLAWLESS

"All the elements of a really good story make this one a keeper...put aside your book markers because you won't need them; turn off the phone because you won't want to be interrupted; lock the door and enjoy this one by Jana Richards."

~*Seriously Reviewed*

~*~

"I was sucked into it in order to find out what happened to Madeleine and Hunter...very intense story involving the Nazis and a ruthless general... revenge and redemption and finding love again...a well written, intense, believable love story."

~*You Gotta Read Reviews*

~*~

BURNING LOVE

"Well-developed and believable...settings and situations were realistic...a delightful book, one easy to recommend."

~*Bitten by Books*

~*~

"Fun and humorous story...I'd love to get to know her and her writing much better."

~*Night Owl Reviews*

Dedication

To my husband Warren
For his unfailing support and love.

Chapter One

Dear Fellow Alumni,

Hard to believe it's been 25 years since we last walked the halls of Summerville High. Wouldn't you like to know what's going on with former classmates?

Cara McLeod shook her head. High school felt like a lifetime ago. Best it remained in the past with the rest of the things she'd left behind, like her marriage.

And her waistline.

The Reunion Committee has worked hard to plan a fabulous, fun-filled three day celebration on the last weekend in June at the historic Summerville Inn. Bring your spouse or come stag. You won't believe the surprises waiting for you!

Surprises? The plugged toilet and her car's dead battery had been all the surprises she could handle this week, thank you very much. After stuffing the invitation into the pocket of her hoodie, Cara turned her attention back to her job and consulted her clipboard. The personal trainer was first up.

As a junior assistant, her job on the local events show at WBST television was to ensure all guests were present and accounted for, provided with coffee and snacks, and escorted onto the sound stage at the appropriate time. Though the guests were adults, in age anyway, the job was a lot like her previous work experience—motherhood. Keep an eagle eye on her charges at all times, feed and water when necessary, and lead them by the hand to wherever they needed to go. As she headed to the green room to retrieve the trainer, she wondered if her ex-husband would attend this fancy shindig of a reunion.

She tried to push thoughts of Peter from her mind, but they stuck like stubborn carpet stains. What did she care if he flaunted his latest young, skinny girlfriend in front of all their old friends? She didn't need a reunion to remind her that few of her high school dreams had come to fruition. She should have left the stupid invitation in the mailbox this morning.

As she opened the door to the green room, Finn Cooper, the personal trainer, rose from his chair and smiled. For the first time Cara realized how tall he was. Not to mention how Adonis-like. "It's show time, Mr. Cooper. I'll take you to the stage now." She looked around the empty room. "Where's the other guest, the chef?"

He cocked his head toward the closed door that led into a washroom. "He looked a little green earlier. He made a dash to the washroom a while ago and hasn't come out."

Great. The last time they'd lost a guest, the director nearly had a breakdown. She gave what she hoped looked like a smile of confidence. "I'm sure he'll be just fine. Let's get you to the sound stage."

She escorted Mr. Cooper to the set, where Jessica Frampton, the perky blonde host of *Rochester Noon,* took one look at the hunky trainer and latched onto his arm like a barnacle. He was on his own; Cara had bigger worries. Hurrying back to the green room, she checked the clipboard for the chef's name before knocking on the washroom door. "Hello? Are you all right in there, Mr. Bricker?"

Through the wooden door, she heard a low moan. "I'm sick. Leave me alone."

"Mr. Bricker, are you too ill to appear on camera?"

"Damned sushi! I don't know whether to sit on the toilet or stick my head in it."

Cara quickly processed that mental picture. The last thing the show needed was a guest barfing on the host—though it would be the most excitement they'd had on the set in months.

"I want to go home."

"Don't worry, Mr. Bricker. We'll look after you."

She hurried back to the set and found the director. "Bill, we've got a problem." She told him about the chef holed up in the washroom.

A fine sheen of perspiration broke out on his forehead. "That's just great. Do we have any other guests lined up for today?"

"Just the personal trainer."

Sitting next to Finn Cooper on the set's sofa, Jessica leaned suggestively, batted perfectly made-up blue eyes in his direction and offered a close-up view of cleavage. Cara grinned while Cooper made a valiant attempt to keep his gaze focused on Jessica's face.

Bill started to pace, mopping his sweaty brow with a handkerchief as he marched. "How are we going to fill an entire hour with one guest? Jessica isn't capable of winging it for that long. She has enough trouble interviewing when we provide her with the questions."

Glad it wasn't her problem, Cara patted his arm. "I'm sure you'll think of something. I'll take care of sending the chef home."

She called a taxi, then escorted Chef Bricker to the front door of the station when it arrived. After assisting their ill guest into the backseat, she handed him a plastic bucket, just in case. By the time she returned to the sound stage, a commercial break had been called.

"There she is!" Jessica shouted.

Bill grabbed her arm and dragged her toward the stage. "Quick Cara, the commercial's almost over."

"Wait!" she yelped, digging in her heels the harder Bill dragged. "What's going on? What are you doing?"

"No time to explain. You're going to be our live example of what people can expect when they visit a personal trainer."

Her stomach pitched. Panic swirled. "*Me* on live TV? No way!"

"You're wearing workout gear today," Jessica gushed. "It's perfect."

Embarrassment heated Cara's cheeks as she glanced down at her sweatpants, T-shirt, and hoodie. She didn't even want to think about the state of her hair. "My washing machine broke down. I ran out of clean clothes." A snapping noise drew her attention to the trainer who held what looked like a giant set of tweezers in his hand. "What is he going to do with *that*?"

"Don't be such a baby." Jessica pulled her up on to the stage. "It's for the show. Take one for the team."

Cara wrenched her arm away. "*You* take one for the team. You get paid more than me."

The floor manager called out, "And we're live in three, two, one..."

Cara froze as Jessica aimed her hundred-watt smile at the camera. "Welcome back to *Rochester Noon*. I'm

Jessica Frampton and we're here today with personal trainer Finn Cooper, who is talking with us about nutrition and fitness." She turned the bright smile on their guest. "Finn, if someone like WBST staffer Cara, who's joined us here, were to go to your gym and set up an appointment, what can she expect to happen?"

Finn shot Cara a worried glance, then cleared his throat. "The first thing we would do is to have her fill out a medical history form. Based on that information, we may ask Cara to consult with her doctor before engaging in any kind of weight loss or exercise program."

"Assuming she is in reasonably good health for someone her age, what happens next?

Cara ground her teeth at the "someone her age" crack. She took a lot of ribbing for being, at forty-three, the oldest junior assistant at the station.

"Then I'd compile personal information, such as current height, weight, build, and body mass index." He handed Jessica a small booklet. "I would also ask that she keep a diary on the food she eats and exercise she gets for a week. That way I get an idea of what her current exercise regime and nutrition habits look like."

"I see you've brought one of the tools of your trade," Jessica said, indicating the giant tweezers in his hand. "What does this instrument do?"

"Calipers like these measure body fat. I take skin-fold measurements from different parts of the body, like the upper arm and the waist, then use these measurements to calculate body fat percentages."

Jessica's eye lit with pure, evil delight. "Why don't we try the calipers on Cara? As a demonstration for our audience, of course."

Cara glared at Jessica, but said nothing. When she looked up into his face, Cooper offered her an apologetic smile. *Yeah, very helpful. Thanks a lot.*

"Stand up and take off that big, bulky hoodie," Jessica directed. "Finn won't be able to get an accurate reading with all that material in the way."

There was a reason she wore the oversize hoodie. It covered the spare tire Jessica was so anxious to measure. She slowly rose to her feet and unzipped the sweatshirt, closing her eyes as she pulled her arms from the sleeves and handed the garment to Finn. Between the fitness hunk and most of the greater Rochester viewing audience, she'd never felt so naked and exposed, even if she was fully clothed.

Finn placed the calipers at her waist and closed the two sections together, trapping a healthy dollop of fat. She cringed, her face heating with embarrassment once more. He handed her the hoodie and she quickly slipped it back on.

"Oh dear, that's quite a lot of fat," Jessica said, shaking her head. "So, Finn, is there anything we can do to help her?"

Is there anything we can do to help her? Jessica made her sound like a beached whale. Next she'd be calling Greenpeace.

Finn arched an eyebrow. "Of course. I'd design a diet and exercise regime tailored specifically for her."

"I understand you've brought with you today the questionnaire you have new clients fill out. Why don't we ask Cara a few of the questions?"

"All right." Finn glanced at her as if gauging her reaction. She lifted her chin a notch. He gave an imperceptible nod. "What do you do for exercise?"

"Ahh, well, not very much."

If she were honest, the biggest exercise of her day was getting up from the couch to get a snack from the fridge.

"Are you able to walk a city block?"

Only if there's an ice-cream shop at the end of it.
"Yes, of course."

Finn shuffled through the pages of his questionnaire. "Have you ever been told you have high blood pressure?"

"No." *But much more of this, and my head will explode.*

"How about your diet? Do you eat eight to ten fruits and vegetables daily?"

Does ketchup count?

"No, probably not."

"Do you have any favorite sports or physical activities that you currently engage in, or that you engaged in at one time?"

Finally, a question she could truthfully answer. "Dancing. I used to love to dance. And way back in high school, I was on the cross country team. I liked running, though I haven't done it in years."

They went through several more embarrassingly personal questions until Jessica changed the subject. "I understand that in addition to having your clients fill out the questionnaire you also conduct a short fitness test at the beginning of the assessment process."

Cara didn't trust the gleam in her eye. What was she up to?

Finn nodded. "It's important to understand the person's basic fitness level."

"Why don't you demonstrate some of these tests

for our audience, Finn?" Jessica patted Cara's shoulder as if she were her best friend. "I'm sure Cara won't mind playing guinea pig."

He looked from her to Jessica and back again, his brow wrinkled in a worried frown. "As long as she's okay with it."

All eyes turned to her. If it were truly up to Cara, she'd run screaming from the room. Instead, she pasted a cheery smile on her face. "Yes, of course."

"All right then. The first thing I want to determine is flexibility. Can you bend from the waist and touch your toes?"

Cara obediently complied, or at least she tried to. Her hands hung in mid-air, somewhere around her knees. She knew that at one time she could certainly touch her toes. In high school she'd been part of the cheerleading squad. Back then, with the flexibility of a rubber band, she'd performed back flips, front walkovers, split leaps, and all manner of gymnastic and dance moves.

But that was twenty-five years ago, according to the invitation stuffed in her pocket.

"For the second test, we need to see how much endurance our client is starting with. We usually use a step machine or a treadmill for that test, so we won't be able to demonstrate here."

"Perhaps we can improvise," Jessica said with a perky smile. "What if Cara did jumping jacks to test her endurance?"

What if Cara smacked Jessica with the calipers?

"Or maybe jumping jacks are too strenuous for someone her age. I wouldn't want her to injure herself." Jessica gave her a smile syrupy enough to throw a diabetic into a coma. "If she can't do them, I understand."

That did it. "No problem at all, Jessica," she said.

"Cara, perhaps—"

"No problem, Finn."

She assumed the classic jumping-jack pose, arms out at shoulder height, legs spread wide. Then she hopped on both feet, bringing her arms to her sides and her legs together. She jumped again and again, inhaling in great gasping breaths. Her knees creaked as she landed. Body parts she'd once thought solid began to move. If she was going to keep this up, she'd definitely need to buy a more supportive bra.

When did she get so out of shape?

"That's enough, Cara," Finn said with a smile. He was probably afraid she'd have a heart attack, live on TV. So was she.

Hair escaped from the clip on the top of her head and clung to her face in sweaty tendrils. She pushed it out of her eyes with an impatient swipe. A stage hand standing just outside camera range signaled to Jessica. Cara narrowed her eyes. Did he have what she thought he had in his hands?

"Here we go," Jessica enthused. "A most essential tool for determining how much weight Cara will need to lose. A scale."

She was about to be weighed on camera, in front of everyone she worked with. The whole city of Rochester, New York would soon know that her weakness for taco chips had resulted in a lot of heavy junk in her trunk. Her only solace was that the ratings for Jessica's show had slipped lately. With any luck, nobody was watching.

The stage hand placed the scale directly in front of Cara, then scurried off. She stared at it, wondering where they'd found one in the TV station. Jessica probably kept it in her dressing room for emergency humiliations.

With a deep breath, she prepared to get on the scale. Maybe, like pulling off a bandage, it was best to get it over with fast. She lifted her foot.

Finn put a hand on her arm to stop her. She looked up at him in confusion.

"Actually, Jessica, I prefer not to use a bathroom scale such as this because they can be notoriously inaccurate. At the gym we use a professional scale, similar to the kind used in doctors' offices, so our clients can be assured our measurement techniques are accurate."

Cara threw a grateful smile to Finn; he responded with a slight nod. Jessica pursed her lips, looking less than pleased. "Fine, we'll skip that part. Anyway, I see that our time is up for today. Thank you for joining us, Finn. Viewers interested in reaching Finn Cooper for their own personal fitness assessment can call him at the New Directions Gym. Goodbye, everyone. We'll see you tomorrow."

The theme music played. A moment later Bill called, "We're out, people. We made it to the end of the show!"

He shook Finn's hand, pumping it vigorously. "Thank you so much for helping us out. We'd be happy to have you as a guest on the show again any time."

"Thank you. I appreciate that."

Jessica put her hand on his arm. "I want to extend my *personal* invitation to you, Finn. Please, anytime you'd like to promote your business again, give me a call."

She handed him one of her business cards. "Listen, I'm nearly done for the day. Why don't you stick around and we can go out for a drink later?"

Finn gave her a polite smile. "I'm sorry, but I have to meet a client at the gym."

"That's too bad. Another time, perhaps?"

"Perhaps," he answered with a noncommittal smile.

Cara hid her grin. Apparently the gorgeous personal trainer wasn't interested in vapid blondes. Her appreciation for the man's taste went up considerably. She walked away, gripping the hair clip between her front teeth as she worked her thick hair into a top knot.

"Cara?"

She almost swallowed the clip when Finn tapped her shoulder. Her hair fell around her face and into her eyes. She pushed it out of the way as she whirled around. "Yes?"

"Are you okay?"

"I'm fine, thanks. A little sweaty and out of breath, but otherwise all right."

"That's good. I'm sorry about the exercises. I know you were unprepared."

Was "unprepared" a euphemism for desperately out of shape?

"Hey, anything for the show. You know how glamorous TV is."

Finn chuckled, and a dimple showed in his chiseled cheek. Cara stared at it, mesmerized. He was an incredibly good-looking man, with dark wavy hair, a long, straight nose, and an exquisitely shaped mouth.

And those stunning blue eyes, which at the moment were regarding her with warm interest.

"I wanted to say thanks for being such a good sport, and to give you this." He handed her a pamphlet. "This entitles you to a free consultation with me at the gym. Make an appointment at your convenience."

Yet again her face heated with embarrassment. What she'd interpreted as personal interest was actually a sales pitch. *Give your head a shake, Cara.* A man as attractive as Finn Cooper would never be interested in her as anything but a client. Besides, he had to be ten years younger than she was, and she'd been dangerously close to making a fool of herself. She forced a smile. "Thank you. I appreciate the offer."

Hell would freeze over before she'd engage the services of Finn Cooper.

Chapter Two

As soon as Cara got home, she pulled the invitation from her pocket and tossed it onto the kitchen counter, intending to throw it into the trash. Even thinking about attending this reunion caused a ball of anxiety to take up residence in the pit of her stomach.

Her thirteen-year-old daughter, Beth, swept into the kitchen, scooping up the envelope. "This is so great, Mom! Dad's going, too. Maybe you can dance together and reminisce about old times in high school when you were dating."

Before she could say there was no way in hell she would "reminisce" with her ex-husband, seventeen-year-old Jenna entered the room and beat her to the punch. "Forget it, Beth. Dad's bringing his new 'friend.'" She put air quotes around the word and rolled her eyes. "He plans to show off his latest hot girlfriend for his old buddies."

The reminder of her ex-husband's penchant for girlfriends almost half his age reopened a wound in Cara's heart that had never truly healed. In Peter's mind, Cara's biggest sin was turning forty. That, and not maintaining her once-trim figure. Three years earlier, on her fortieth birthday, he announced he wanted a divorce.

"I need more than this," he'd said. "I don't want to spend the rest of my life worrying about mortgages and soccer. I want to experience life. I want to have some fun! And quite frankly, I'm not attracted to you anymore."

Then he left. *Happy birthday, Cara.*

"I think I'd rather stay home with you guys." Beth looked so crestfallen at the news, Cara drew her into a hug. She could forgive Peter for what he'd done to her, but she'd never forget the pain he'd caused their daughters. "Maybe we'll have a girls' night out, go to dinner and a movie together."

"I told Dad you were going to the reunion," Jenna said.

Heart sinking, Cara stared at her oldest daughter. On the outside Jenna appeared to have taken the divorce and the resulting move to a tiny condo in stride. But Cara knew her daughter kept all her anger locked up, showing the world an I-don't-give-a-damn face.

Maybe she'd learned that little trick from her mother.

"Why would you tell Dad that?"

"Because he laughed."

"Laughed? What do you mean?"

"He said he was taking the hottest girl to the reunion and all the other men would be jealous. And then I said that wasn't possible because he wasn't taking you. That's when he laughed."

Jenna inhaled deeply, holding back tears. "He said maybe twenty-five years ago that was true, but not anymore. I was so mad I told him you were going and furthermore you would be the hottest girl at the reunion."

Though Cara's pride took a direct hit at Jenna's words, she'd survive. What she couldn't tolerate was

Peter's callous treatment of his daughter. Didn't he realize how sensitive she was? Didn't he know that making fun of her mother forced Jenna to take sides in a loyalty contest? It was a choice no child should have to make.

Cara reached out to her, struggling to keep the anger out of her voice. "Forget about it, honey. We'll just stay home and—"

"No!" Jenna jerked away. "I'm tired of Dad saying mean things about you, and I'm tired of you taking it. Don't you care?"

"You're the one who's mean, Jenna!" Beth cried. "Dad would never say nasty things about Mom! He loves her! I know he does!"

"Open your eyes, Beth! They'll never get back together, so forget about it."

Cara's heart cried for both girls. She'd known Jenna was hurting, but she hadn't realized how much. And did Beth really think she and Peter would get back together? "Girls, stop it! We'll talk about this later. Right now we need to get to Beth's soccer game."

Jenna threw her an indecipherable look before heading to the front door. Cara kissed Beth once more, then gently pushed her toward the door. "Go get your cleats. We're going to be late."

After Beth went to her room, Cara picked up the invitation once more, Jenna's words echoing in her ears. *Don't you care?*

Did she care that her husband had abandoned her, flaunting his young girlfriends in her face? Did she care that her daughters were hurting and feeling abandoned as well? Did she care that she'd put Peter through dental school, setting aside her own career ambitions?

Did she care that she'd gained twenty-five pounds in the last five years, making her feel frumpy, fat, and over forty?

Hell yeah, she cared! She cared a lot.

The question was, what was she going to do about it?

****

"So go," Cara's friend, Nancy Armstrong, said. "Buy yourself a hot mama dress, go to this stupid reunion, and show the world what a jerk Peter is for leaving you."

"It's not so simple."

Cara shaded her eyes against the glare. She'd forgotten her sunglasses again, and had to squint as she watched Beth take a penalty kick against the opposing goalkeeper.

Great. All she needed were more lines around her eyes.

"Why are you making this so difficult? Just go." Nancy stood and clapped. "Woo-hoo! Way to go, Beth! Nice job, girls!"

Cara stood and cheered for Beth's goal as well. She and Nancy had been friends since they met at their daughters' soccer practice eight years earlier. They'd stuck together through Nancy's divorce, then Cara's, leaning on one another for support and encouragement.

"I don't want to embarrass myself."

Nancy resumed her seat. "Are you planning to get drunk and dance on the tables? Maybe do a little strip tease? You never could hold your liquor."

"Very funny."

"Honey, it's a twenty-five-year reunion. I know it's hard to believe, but everyone will have aged, not just you. And everyone will have gained a few pounds. I don't think the invitation stipulated that you had to be your exact high school weight in order to attend."

The trouble with having a friend who knew her so well was that she knew her so well. Nancy wouldn't let her off the hook until she spilled every last bit of it.

"I know it sounds really vain and petty, but back in high school I was voted the girl most likely. The girl most likely to have her picture on the cover of *Vogue*, the girl most likely to be the CEO of a Fortune 500 company. The girl most likely to have the perfect marriage. Everyone thought big things would happen for me. So did I."

Cara had been class president in her junior year, editor of the yearbook, captain of the cheerleading squad. She and Peter had been the golden couple all through high school, and married a year after they graduated. She'd dropped out of college to support them so that he could concentrate on his dentistry studies. He'd promised that when he finished school, she'd have her chance. But by the time he'd graduated, Cara was pregnant with Jenna and earning her degree was no longer a priority.

Immediately after the divorce, with money from the settlement, she'd enrolled in the University of Rochester's economics department, hoping to someday earn an MBA like she'd always planned. But she soon realized she no longer knew what she wanted to be when she grew up. And she felt out of place in a world geared to twenty-year-olds. After a year she dropped out, deciding to get a job and work until she figured things out.

She soon discovered there wasn't a lot of call for

forty-something workers with no real training for anything other than child care and throwing a really great dinner party. Her work experience consisted of waiting on tables and selling clothes in a boutique. She'd been lucky to get the entry level position at WBST, although it made her the oldest living gopher in the world.

Nancy pulled a bag of sunflower seeds from her purse and offered some to Cara. "You've done the biggest thing of all—raised two kids virtually single-handed into confident, smart young women. With hardly an obnoxious bone in their bodies."

Cara stuck her hand in the bag and grabbed a fistful of seeds. "I'm not so sure about the confident part. I'm just starting to realize how hard the divorce has been on them." She told Nancy about the confrontation before the game.

"Maybe they're taking their cue from you."

"What do you mean?"

Nancy sighed, then turned her attention back to the game, clapping when her daughter Chrissy scored another goal. "What kind of message do you think you're sending your girls when you won't attend your own high school reunion because you've gained weight?"

"That's not why I'm not going!"

"Isn't it? Honey, do you want your daughters to believe their worth is tied directly to their attractiveness to men? Don't you want them to be proud of their accomplishments?"

"Of course I do." Was she really teaching her girls that they were only worthwhile if they were a perfect size two? "But Peter said—"

"Forget about Peter." Nancy made a face at the mention of Cara's ex. "You've spent way too much time obsessing over him these last three years. It's time to get on with your life, date other men."

"Please," Cara scoffed. "The last thing I need is another man."

"You're judging the entire male species by Peter's dismal performance. Believe it or not, there are some decent guys out there."

Finn Cooper's face immediately popped to mind. He seemed like a decent guy, even if his only real interest in her was as a paying customer. And she couldn't deny he was easy on the eyes. Whoever coined the phrase "buns of steel" was looking at him.

She'd never been with anyone but Peter, never even dated another man. The thought of starting a new relationship terrified her. And the idea of getting naked with another man made her shudder. Good lord, except to shower, she didn't get naked when she was alone. No way would she strip down for anyone else, particularly a perfect human specimen like Finn Cooper.

Even so, she had to admit her double bed was getting very lonely.

"I can't stand the thought of everyone at the reunion either feeling sorry for me or laughing behind my back because I've lost my perfect figure and my perfect life didn't turn out so perfect." She sighed. "I was so conceited in high school. I was a pretty girl and I made sure everybody knew it. All I was interested in was being accepted by the popular kids and doing everything they did. I wasn't always a very nice person."

She thought of Mitzi Goldberg, her chemistry lab

partner. Mitzi was an outgoing girl with thick glasses, short in stature but long on brains. Ms. Brainiac, Cara called her. Mitzi's wickedly sharp sense of humor was often aimed at the most popular girls, including Cara's fellow cheerleaders. Despite their different outlooks on life, she liked her. But Mitzi didn't fit into narrowly defined parameters of what was considered popular back in high school. And Peter had never liked her, probably because with a few well-chosen words, she could slice him down to her own diminutive size.

Cara dropped Mitzi as a friend, but now she wondered whatever had happened to her.

"You're being too hard on yourself," Nancy said. "You were just a kid, a stupid kid. All of us make mistakes in high school."

"You're far more charitable than I deserve."

She knew she hadn't always been the best person. Perhaps she'd become that way because back then, everything—boys, grades, and compliments—had come so easily. Hard times had given her a whole new perspective on life, along with a lot more compassion, tolerance and humility.

"I dread the thought of showing up at this reunion twenty-five pounds overweight, divorced, and working in an entry-level job. I thought I was going to set the world on fire." Cara shook her head in disgust. "I've barely lit a match."

"You feel like a failure."

She couldn't look her friend in the eye. "Yes."

"So what are you going to do about it?"

"Do? I don't know. What do you think I should do?"

"It doesn't matter what I think. The only person

whose opinion matters is you. What do you have to do to not feel like a failure?"

Cara still pondered that question when she and the girls arrived home. The phone was ringing as they opened the door. She checked the call display and groaned; her mother was calling from Florida. For a brief moment she considered letting the call go to message, but she knew her mother would simply keep phoning until she got an answer. With a sigh, she picked up the phone. *Might as well get this over with.*

"Hi, Mom. How are you?"

"Dreadful. It's unbearably hot here today. Why your father insists on staying in Florida through the sweltering summers, I'll never understand. What took you so long to answer the phone?"

Cara stifled a sigh. Just once she'd like to have a pleasant conversation with her mother. "We only this minute stepped into the house. Beth had a soccer game."

"Soccer." Mariette Blackwell said the word as if it were something dirty. "Such an unladylike game. Why don't you have my granddaughters involved in more feminine pursuits like piano or ballet?"

They'd been through this so many times. "The girls like soccer. I'm kind of busy, Mom. Was there something specific you wanted?"

"Actually, there was. My friend Latisha Price in Summerville phoned to say she saw you on television today, on the TV show you work for. She said you looked positively unkempt. She also said you've put on even more weight since she last saw you. What on earth is going on with you, Cara? Have you no pride in your appearance?"

So much for no one watching *Rochester Noon.* Apparently they were big in the snooty-over-sixty-five demographic. "No, Mom, I have no pride left whatsoever. It's been lovely talking to you, but I really have to go—"

"If you hadn't divorced Peter, you wouldn't need to work."

More old territory. "I told you, Mom. Peter left me. It wasn't like I had a whole lot of choice in the matter."

"I don't know why you had to give up your beautiful house. How can you entertain guests in that tiny condo of yours?"

"I like my condo, and the only guests we entertain these days are Jenna and Beth's friends." Sometimes she missed the house she'd shared with Peter, with its gourmet kitchen, swimming pool, and palatial master suite. But after he left she wanted a new start. The condo wasn't huge, but it was easy to clean, close to the girls' school, and best of all, it was totally hers.

"Perhaps if you hadn't let yourself go you could have maintained his interest."

She'd definitely need an antacid after this conversation. "Mom, I'm tired. If you've said your piece, I'm going to say goodnight."

"Fine." Mariette sounded as if she had plenty more to say. Cara had no doubt she'd hear much more on the subject of her weight. "Give my granddaughters my love."

Her love. Right. "Of course. Goodnight."

"Goodnight."

Cara set the handset back on its cradle, her hand trembling and her stomach tied in knots. Why did she let her mother get to her like this?

Even after tidying the condo and making lunches for the next day, she couldn't get her conversation with her mother out of her head. Nancy's words came back to her. *What do you have to do to not feel like a failure?*

Making enough money so she didn't need to rely on Peter's child support and alimony would be one way. Getting her mother off her back would be another. Showing her daughters strength, courage, and determination was the ultimate failure-busting goal.

In the privacy of her bedroom, she took a deep breath and stripped off all her clothes. Her inner cheerleader cringed when she felt the ring of pudge circling her waist, and the extra layer of fat covering her hips and butt. In the six weeks until the reunion she couldn't become a high-rolling executive making a six-figure salary. But she might be able to prove to the girls that she wasn't afraid to face their father or her past by attending the reunion. She might even be able to lose a few pounds by then, perhaps enough to satisfy her mother. Maybe enough to fit into the dress she'd bought herself on her fortieth birthday in a last ditch attempt to make Peter think she was still sexy.

Grabbing her old robe, she hurried into the living room to find the hoodie she'd worn to work. She found it in the closet, and searched the pockets for the pamphlet she'd stowed inside. The crumpled paper confirmed that it entitled the holder to a free fitness evaluation with Finn Cooper. The slogan caught her eye: *If you're ready to find a new you, I'm here to show you the way.*

Cara was so ready.

Alert the papers. Hell had just frozen over.

Chapter Three

Cara entered the gym like a soldier stepping into hostile territory. She tried to recall the last time she'd been at a gym and came up with—never. Until five years ago she'd never felt the need to work out. Now she wished she'd said no to a few desserts and yes to more walks in the park.

"I'm here to see Finn Cooper," she told the attractive young woman at the reception desk. "I have a 5:30 appointment."

The blue-eyed blonde consulted her computer. "You must be Cara McLeod. After you fill out these forms, I'll call Finn for you." As she handed over a clipboard and pen, Cara noted the blonde's toned arms. Unlike her own arms, no flesh sagged like kimono sleeves flapping in the breeze. "Let me know when you've finished with the forms."

Cara took the clipboard and sat in the waiting area. The first form was straight forward. Name, rank, serial number, waiver absolving the gym of liability if she should injure herself due to her own stupidity. The next form contained some of the questions Finn had asked her on *Rochester Noon*, things about her diet and how much she currently exercised. But other questions cut to the heart of her motivation for coming to the gym.

What are your reasons for seeking a personal trainer?

Cara answered, "To become more fit and healthy." True as far as it went.

If you are here to lose weight, what are your reasons?

She wrote, "To gain confidence and energy." Again, it was true—partially. She really didn't want to get into a discussion about her insecurities and failures.

How much weight do you want to lose? Simple. Twenty-five pounds.

How will losing weight change your life? This one threw her. Her life wouldn't magically improve if she lost twenty-five pounds. She'd still be working the same old job, living in the same tiny condo, and dealing with the same self-centered ex-husband and hypercritical mother. But perhaps losing weight would make her feel more like her old self again. Maybe she could get back her mojo.

"If I lose weight, I'll feel like me again*,"* she wrote.

"Great!" the perky blonde receptionist said when Cara handed the clipboard back. "Finn will be with you in a couple of minutes."

She sat once more. From the waiting area she saw a row of stationary bikes, each occupied by a rider peddling as madly as a gerbil running its wheel. For people going nowhere fast, they certainly appeared determined.

"Hi, Cara. It's good to see you again."

When she'd met him at the station, she'd compared Finn to the Greek god Adonis. But seeing him again, she realized she'd been wrong. The six feet of hard-bodied, well-muscled male standing in front of her was far superior to any mythical god or marble statue. She swallowed nervously as she reached for the hand he extended to her. Had she remembered to put on deodorant this morning?

"It's good to see you, too."

"To tell you the truth, I didn't think you'd use the free assessment, but I'm glad you did." He continued to hold her hand, even though they'd passed the greeting portion of the conversation. She gently tugged her hand free.

"I guess you could tell that diet and exercise haven't been a big priority in my life for some time. The massive amount of fat you trapped in your calipers might have given you a hint."

Finn winced. "I feel awful about that interview. I never should have agreed to go ahead with it. You were totally blindsided."

"Don't give it another thought. I'm totally over it." *You're such a liar, Cara.*

"Good. Well, anyway, you're here now. Why don't you follow me to my office? We'll discuss the information on your forms and figure out where we go from here."

She followed him through the gym. The scents of sweat and testosterone hovered in the air. Weights clanged as hard-muscled men and women bench pressed the equivalent of a Buick. What the hell was she doing here? She felt like an alien, a misfit. The Sesame Street song "One of These Things is Not Like the Others" played in her head.

At last, they reached a small office and Finn motioned for her to have a seat across the desk from him while he perused her paperwork. Cara checked out his office. Books lined up neatly on a shelf behind the desk. Diplomas and certificates hung on the wall in a precise row. Even the stapler and paper clip dispenser on his desk stood at attention. She wished her condo looked this organized.

Finn looked up from the paperwork. "You say on your form that you'd like to lose twenty-five pounds. That's a reasonable goal. We can set up an exercise regime for you, get you started on a healthy, low-fat, low-calorie diet. My aim for you will be a weight loss of two pounds a week."

"Two pounds a week?" She did the math. There were just five and a half weeks left until the reunion. At that rate, the most she could lose was ten pounds, eleven max. "Isn't there a way we can jump start the weight loss? Perhaps a more stringent diet, or increased exercise?"

"I understand the desire to get rid of the weight quickly, but if you lose the pounds slowly, you're more likely to keep them off," Finn explained. His brow furrowed as he looked into her face. "Crash diets rarely work for long. If you figure out how to incorporate exercise and healthy eating into your daily routine, the weight will stay off."

"I need to lose the entire twenty-five pounds in five and a half weeks! Isn't there something we can do?"

"Why do you *need* to lose twenty-five pounds in five and a half weeks?" When she said nothing, he leaned forward in his chair, his eyes shining with empathy. "I really do understand your desire to lose weight. You feel guilty and stupid for letting your weight get out of hand. You're uncomfortable in your own skin, embarrassed. But you don't need to embarrassed with me. Maybe if you tell me what really motivated you to come here today, I can help you figure out where we go from here."

She considered lying or giving him a flippant answer, but the kindness in his blue eyes encouraged her to tell the truth. "I'm going to my high school reunion and I don't want to be fat." Once the confession began, she couldn't stop. "My ex-husband is going to be there with his skinny young girlfriend, and I don't want to look like a blimp. I'm tired of feeling like crap, and I'm tired of my daughters seeing me defeated and unhappy. I don't want to feel like a loser anymore!"

While Cara blushed madly, Finn simply nodded. The look in his eyes made her believe he really did know how she felt, though how someone as gorgeous as Finn could know what it was like to be fat and unattractive, she had no clue.

"I'll make you a deal," he said. "For the first two weeks of your program we'll restrict the number of carbs you eat. That should jump start a weight loss for you. At the same time, we'll gradually build up the intensity of your workouts. But after this class reunion is over, you have to go back to sensible eating and exercising."

Relief made her almost giddy. "Thanks, Finn, I will, but just to be clear, I only plan to use your services until the reunion is over. After that I'll work out on my own."

"Fair enough. Just promise me you won't go crazy with the dieting. It's not good for business if my clients drop dead from lack of nourishment."

Cara held up three fingers of her right hand in the Girl Scout salute. "I promise I'll do everything you say. When can we start?"

His smile took her breath away. "No time like the present."

****

Finn led Cara into the room where the scale was located. He saw her frown at the machine as if it were an instrument of torture. He could sympathize. There was a time when he'd hated the bloody thing himself.

"I haven't weighed myself in a long time." She closed her eyes a moment, her hands forming fists at her sides. "I guess this is the moment of truth."

"It's just a number, Cara. It doesn't mean anything. What's more important is feeling healthy and energetic and full of confidence. All the scale does is tell us how close we're getting to where we want to be."

She looked up at him, her mouth turned down in a skeptical frown. "I'll try to keep that in mind when the scale rips me to shreds."

He'd have his work cut out for him with this one. Half the trick to losing weight was believing it was possible, but Cara was not yet a believer. "Are you ready?"

"As I'll ever be." She took a deep breath and exhaled slowly before stepping on the scale. Finn adjusted the weights to get an accurate reading.

"There. That's not so bad, is it?"

"It's a lot more than what I weighed in high school."

"What isn't different from high school? Would you really want to be the same person you were back then?"

For a moment Cara stared at him. Then suddenly, her lips curved into a smile that transformed her face, like the sun emerging through the clouds. "No, I definitely would not want to be the same person I was in high school."

For the first time since arriving at the gym, she looked at ease. He couldn't help smiling back at her. "Come on. Let's get those measurements done."

Finn found a tape in a drawer and instructed Cara on how to stand and where to place the tape on her body. Taking measurements required close contact. The light floral scent of her perfume and the silkiness of her skin caused an unexpected reaction in his body. *Is it getting hot in here?*

Sweat prickled his back and underarms and, to his horror, he felt an erection stirring to life. He frowned as he noted her bust measurement—forty inches—in her file. He'd weighed and measured dozens of female clients without having hormones get in the way. Why was Cara different?

"So, what's the verdict, Doctor?"

He slammed shut the manila file folder as if it was about to rat on him for his lack of professionalism. Taking a couple of steps away from her, he willed his body to behave. "You'll live. Come with me, and we'll determine your fitness level."

It soon became obvious that he had his work cut out for him with Cara's workouts, along with her attitude. She struggled with even the smallest free weights. Her upper body strength was nonexistent, and though he'd already witnessed how little endurance she possessed after the jumping jacks debacle, it was even worse than he'd thought. Sweat rolled down her face as she peddled the stationary bike.

"Are…we…there…yet?" she panted.

"Just three more minutes. You can do it."

"Are you sure about that?" She groaned. "My legs

have turned to gelatin, my heart is going to jump out of my chest, and my lungs are about to explode. I haven't got three more minutes!"

He was losing her. "Close your eyes, Cara."

"What?"

"Just close your eyes. We're doing a visualization exercise. Trust me."

She shot him a skeptical glance before lowering her eyelids. "Now what?"

"Picture yourself arriving at your class reunion. Where's it being held?"

"The ballroom at the Summerville Inn."

"You arrive and all eyes are on you. You're wearing a hot dress in an even hotter color, and you look fantastic. You feel great, too. You want to dance all night. You said you used to dance, right?"

"Right." Her forehead wrinkled in concentration. She had beautifully shaped brows and a clear complexion, now flushed with exertion. "Is Peter there?"

"Peter?"

"My ex. Is he there with his little girlfriend?"

"Peter's there, but not with the girlfriend. Her mommy won't let her stay out past curfew."

Cara laughed. The throaty chuckle tickled his libido. He had his own visualization of him pulling her off the bike and kissing her senseless.

"He takes you out onto the dance floor and tells you he was a fool for letting you get away."

"You mean he was a fool for dumping me, don't you?"

"Whatever. He's sorry. But you tell him you've got a new life now, and it doesn't include him."

"I'm liking this visualization thing," she wheezed. "Does he cry?"

"He does if you want him to."

"I want him to cry for his mommy."

"Then he's bawling like a baby."

She pumped one fist in the air. "Who-hoo!"

Finn smiled, enjoying her delight. She was certainly an attractive woman, but not the most beautiful client he'd ever had. Why did he feel such a pull toward her? "Tell me about Peter. How long were you married?"

"Twenty years. We got married shortly after high school. I've known him practically all my life."

Was she still in love with her ex? First love was a powerful thing, and hard to give up on, especially when it gives up on you. "Okay, Cara, three minutes are up. You can stop now."

Her legs immediately stopped churning and she slumped over the handlebars, breathing hard. After a moment she lifted her head, her smile dazzling despite the messy ponytail and the sweat-stained T-shirt. "I can do this, can't I?" she said in wonder. "I'm really going to do this."

Finn's heart turned over. He allowed himself one touch, a brief squeeze to her shoulder. "You bet. I'll make sure of it."

Chapter Four

Two weeks into her fitness regime and progress was slow. Despite working out at the gym four times a week and watching every morsel she ate, Cara almost wept when she'd lost only two pounds. Two lousy pounds! But Finn had talked her off the ledge by reminding her that she'd lost an inch around her waist and a half inch from her abdomen. Of course, she'd also lost a half inch from her bust. Of course.

As she peddled the stationery bike, she watched other members of the gym, especially the women. Each looked strong and confident, and surprisingly stylish. In her baggy T-shirt and the Lycra shorts she'd borrowed from Nancy, she felt like one of Cinderella's ugly stepsisters. After she lost a few more pounds, she'd have to go shopping. Maybe she wasn't in tip-top shape like the others, but at least she could dress the part. Fake it till you make it, she always said.

Despite the dismal weight loss so far, Finn claimed her progress to be excellent, so Cara chose to believe him. He also reminded her that she was building muscle and that muscle weighed more than fat. Though she knew he was right, she couldn't help wishing the numbers on his scale would give her better news.

In the two weeks they'd worked together, he'd treated her in a completely professional manner. After measuring her that first time, he made sure Kate the receptionist handled the task the following weeks. He rarely touched her, except to correct her form while she used the equipment. Cara found herself deliberately making mistakes just so he'd put his hands on her.

How pathetic was that?

She watched him consult her file on his clipboard. "You're doing great, Cara. When we started, you couldn't stay on the bike for more than five minutes. Now you're up to fifteen and you still have energy for the elliptical machine."

"Thanks. I had a good teacher."

"It's been my pleasure to coach you."

For a second their gazes locked and Cara swore she heard electricity crackle in the air, but then he averted his gaze and stepped away. She sighed. Her overactive imagination was playing a game of wishful thinking.

"So are you applying for the new job you told me about?"

"I don't think I've got much of a shot."

A new position in the ad department at the station had opened up. The junior advertising associate helped to dream up creative new ads for local clients. The job meant a pay increase and a step up the career ladder— but with no experience, the station had zero reasons to consider her for the job.

"It doesn't hurt to give it a try. What's the worst they can say?"

"'Hell, no!' is a distinct possibility. It's not like I'm such a prize as an employee."

"Why are you always putting yourself down? You're smart and funny, and if those fools at the TV station can't see that, then to hell with them!"

Cara stared at him, stunned by his vehemence. She

had no idea what to say. Was he angry at her for being a wimp, or at the station for not recognizing her brilliance?

No. It had to be the former.

Embarrassed, she ducked her head. What made her think she could handle a job like that anyway?

"I'm sorry. I didn't mean to upset you. It's just that I hate to see you sell yourself short." He touched her shoulder. "Sweetheart, look at me."

The whispered endearment on Finn's lips had her head snapping up to face him. Her heart pounded, hope blossoming inside her chest.

"I'm sorry. Can you forgive me?"

She would have walked over hot coals if he'd asked. She dredged up a smile. "Of course. There's nothing to forgive."

"Then you'll apply for the job?"

Why did it matter so much to him? "Maybe. I'll think about it."

"Good." He closed his eyes a second. "I can't stand the thought that I hurt you."

"You didn't. I'm fine." She'd been hurt by the best. This didn't even come close. She took his hand. "Honestly. I'm fine."

"Okay." He let go of her hand, once more the poster boy of professionalism. "Stay with the bike for another five minutes and then we'll move on to the weights."

"Aye aye, captain."

Finn gave her a wink. "Just keep working."

He remained playful for the rest of her workout. Cara floated into the ladies' locker room on a wave of happiness.

She finished her shower and was drying off in her stall when she heard two women talking. Cara scarcely paid attention, until she heard, "Did you see the cow eyes she made at Finn?"

She stopped drying and listened intently.

"As if he'd be interested in a woman who's got to be ten years older."

"Have you seen the outfits she wears? Where does she shop? The Salvation Army?"

They laughed uproariously. Shame and embarrassment welled up from the pit of her stomach. They were right. What would a gorgeous younger man like Finn possibly see in a frumpy, overweight woman like her? What a stupid, middle-aged fool she'd been.

She waited until she heard the showers running before she dressed and made her escape. Finn waved at her as she left the locker room.

"Cara, wait. Do you have a minute?"

"Sorry, no. I've got to get home to my daughters. 'Bye."

She ran to her car and drove to a park near her home, then into a parking lot used only by maintenance staff. She pulled her car to a stop between two city trucks, finally feeling alone.

Slumped over the steering wheel, she wept tears of shame that crashed down her cheeks as waves of humiliation engulfed her. Had she been so starved for affection she'd latched on to the fantasy that Finn felt something for her? Maybe Peter had been right. She really was pathetic.

Cara cried until she simply didn't have the energy to cry anymore. Then she blew her nose and wiped her tears in an attempt to repair the red and swollen eyes she saw in the rearview mirror. She didn't want the girls to know what she'd been doing.

She thought about going to Nancy's house but couldn't face the embarrassment of admitting she'd actually thought a younger man found her attractive.

Finally she started her car, adjusted the rearview mirror, and wiped her eyes one last time before heading home.

Nice fantasy while it lasted.

Chapter Five

"Hello, dear. How are you?"

"I'm fine, Mom." Just the person she wanted to talk to after arriving home from her meltdown. She reached for the bottle of Tums in her medicine cabinet. "How are you and Dad?"

"We're feeling much better. There's a lovely breeze coming off the ocean today. Listen, I was talking to one of my friends here, and she was telling me about how her daughter-in-law lost fifty pounds."

Oh Lord. Here it comes.

"Mom, I really don't—"

"She went on the zooni berry diet. Dropped all that weight in less than three months."

"That doesn't sound very healthy."

"And being fifty pounds overweight *is* healthy?"

She opened the bottle and took out two antacid tablets. "I'm not fifty pounds overweight."

"Close to it, from what Latisha Price told me. I can't tell you how embarrassed I was by that phone call."

Cara popped a third Tums into her mouth. "Yes, Mother, I gained weight just to embarrass you."

"Don't be impertinent. I'm trying to help you."

Help me. Right. "Yes, the zooni berry diet. What are zooni berries anyway?"

"A marvelous fruit that comes from someplace

foreign, and they're just bursting with vitamins and antioxidants and things that make you lose weight. My friend's daughter-in-law ate a cup of berries every day for three months and lost fifty pounds."

"If that's all she ate, I'm not surprised."

"She ate other things, in moderation. I'm going to send the information to you. Apparently you can get zooni berries at good health food stores."

"Mom, I'm really not interested—"

"Do you want to be fat for the rest of your life? What man is going to look at you when you're as bloated as a cow?"

She'd thought she'd moved past the point where her mother's jabs could hurt. Occasionally one found its mark. "Fine. Send the information. I have to go now. Goodnight."

"Goodnight, dear." Marietta sounded chipper. But then she would since she'd once more gotten her own way.

She disengaged the call and reached for the Pepto Bismal. When was she ever going to stand up to her mother and tell her to leave her alone?

****

Cara didn't show up for her scheduled workout the next day. Finn thought it strange she didn't call but assumed something had come up.

When she didn't come to the gym the day after that, he began to worry that something had happened. On the following day when he received a terse message saying she no longer required his services, concern turned to anger.

He got her home phone number from the paperwork she'd filled out and gave her a call. A young girl answered the phone. "Hello?"

"Can I speak to Cara, please?"

"Just a minute."

Finn heard a half-muffled voice say, "Mom! Phone for you!" *Pause.* "I don't know who it is." *Pause.* Then the young girl's voice on the line again. "Who's calling, please?"

"It's Finn Cooper."

"Mom, it's Finn Cooper!" *Pause.* "But he's on the phone right now." *Pause.* "That's not very polite." *Pause. Dramatic sigh.* "I'm sorry. My mom says she can't speak to you. Goodbye."

The phone went dead in his hand. What the hell had he done to make her so angry? Had she been that upset by his stupid remark about her always putting herself down?

He tried calling twice more with the same result, different young voice on the phone. Obviously he wasn't going to get through to her by that method, and he was beginning to feel like a stalker.

If he was going to be a stalker he might as well go all the way.

After an evening of debating with himself over the wisdom of his next move, he made his decision. At seven the next morning, he waited in his car outside the neat but unremarkable condo building where Cara and her daughters lived. Was he crazy? Probably, but until he heard a reasonable explanation as to why she'd suddenly quit, he couldn't rest.

From the first time she'd flashed that incredible smile at him, he'd known he'd do anything to help her. Apparently that included surveillance on her house at seven in the morning. Finn shook his head, not sure whether to be amused or alarmed by his uncharacteristic actions.

Cara opened the door to her condo and descended the steps with a sexy sway to her hips, looking like a ray of sunshine in a yellow blouse and a black skirt. Her unbound hair fell in a shiny blonde curtain around her shoulders. Finn's mouth went dry. He'd never seen her in anything but baggy workout clothes, with her hair in a lopsided ponytail. Her modest heels made her long, shapely legs even longer and shapelier. The woman cleaned up good.

He scrambled from his car. "Cara, wait! I need to talk to you."

She froze at the sound of his voice. He stopped a few feet away from her, suddenly not knowing what to say. He'd rehearsed a speech about not giving up on her goals; about how much easier it would be for her to reach her desired weight with his help. But now that he was standing in front of her, all he could think to say was, "I missed you."

Cara blinked a couple of times and looked away. For a long moment she remained silent. When she finally spoke, her voice was so soft Finn barely heard her. "I missed you, too." She added hastily, "I mean, I missed you nagging me to exercise. It's hard to stay motivated on my own."

"Then why did you stop coming to the gym?"

"It wasn't working out." She pulled a pair of sunglasses from her purse and put them on, hiding her eyes from him. "I'll be fine on my own."

"Look, if you're not comfortable coming to the gym, I'll come to you. We'll work out a schedule—"

"No! It's better if we leave things as they are. I've

got to get to work. Goodbye, Finn."

With that she hurried down the street, her heels clicking on the cement sidewalk. Finn watched her leave, his heart torn between despair and hope. Okay, so she said she didn't want to work out with him anymore. But she'd also said she missed him. He hung on to that tiny pearl.

Damn it, he was going to help her whether she liked it or not. He hoped that didn't make him a real stalker. He also hoped he wasn't in way over his head.

****

Damn, she hated carrot sticks.

What she really wanted, Cara thought on a sigh, was a big bag of dill pickle potato chips in all their artificially flavored splendor. Or maybe double chocolate chip ice cream. Or possibly both, at the same time. With sprinkles.

She took another bite of carrot.

Her bathroom scale just confirmed what she'd already suspected; she hadn't lost an ounce since she quit working out at the gym. What was the point of dieting anymore? It wasn't like she'd ever make Peter or any other man salivate over her. Maybe it wasn't too late to back out of the class reunion. She'd only signed up for the dinner and dance on Saturday. Hopefully she could still get her money back.

The doorbell snapped her back to the present. Beth skipped by her to answer it, grabbing a carrot stick as she passed. At least somebody in the house liked them.

"Mom!" Beth re-entered the kitchen, eyes saucer-wide. "Someone's at the door to see you. He's a boy!"

Cara grabbed her purse and headed to the door, stifling a smile. Probably the paperboy looking for payment. Beth was just at the age when she was starting to notice boys and boys were starting to notice her. Her baby was growing up.

"How much do I owe—"

She stopped abruptly. Finn stood unsmiling in the front hallway, his large frame filling her small condo. Unease knotted her stomach. At the same time, her heart sang at the sight of him. She decided to go with her gut.

"What are you doing here?"

"I want to show you something."

"I'm not going back to the gym, so you can save your breath."

"Just hear me out. Please."

By the determined glitter in his eyes, she knew he meant to have his say, one way or another. "Fine," she sighed. "But Jenna's got a soccer game in an hour, so you'll have to make it quick."

"No problem."

"Is everything all right, Mom?"

Jenna moved up beside her and reached for her hand. On her other side, Beth laid her hand on Cara's shoulder. "Everything's fine, honey." Cara put her arm around Jenna's shoulders, using her like a shield between herself and Finn. "Whatever you want to say to me, you'll have to say in front of my daughters. We don't have any secrets from each other, do we, girls?"

He hesitated a moment, swallowed, and then nodded. "Sure. They can hear this."

"All right. I guess I should introduce you then. Girls, this is Finn Cooper, my former personal trainer." She emphasized *former.* "Finn, my daughters, Jenna and Beth."

He held out his hand and smiled, shaking each girl's hand. "Nice to meet you."

"Why don't we move into the living room?"

Cara led the way into their slightly cluttered front room. She pushed some newspapers from the recliner and motioned for Finn to sit. She sat on the sofa across from him, the girls perching on either side of her, their attention glued to him.

"You said you wanted to show me something?"

"Yes." For the first time she noticed that he held a shopping bag and a large brown envelope. He passed the envelope to her. "Open it. There's a picture inside I want you to see."

Cara pulled a picture of a very obese man from the envelope. He looked tired and defeated, hopeless even. Her heart went out to him immediately. "I suppose this is one of your clients and you're going to tell me you helped him lose weight and feel better about himself. I'm very happy for him, but I'm fine. I'll lose weight on my own."

"That's not a client." He looked directly into her eyes. "It's me."

For a moment she didn't know what to say. She looked at the picture once more. The hair color was the same, though the style was different now. And when she examined the face closely she realized she was looking into Finn's glorious blue eyes. But everything else was different. The man in the picture was not only fat, he exuded unhappiness. The man she knew now radiated positive energy.

The continuing silence made her uncomfortable. What was he trying to tell her? How did she respond without embarrassing or hurting him?

"Wow! You were really fat!" Beth said in wide-eyed wonder.

"Beth!"

Finn laughed. "It's all right. Yeah, I was."

"How did you get so fat?" Jenna asked.

Her face heated at her daughter's direct question, but Finn seemed unbothered. "I was always a heavy kid. Everyone in my family is overweight. Some of it is genetic, but mostly it was because I overate and didn't exercise. One day I woke up and I looked like that."

"What made you decide to lose weight?" Jenna asked. Cara listened closely, wanting to know the answer, too.

"Five years ago, just before my thirtieth birthday, I went to the doctor and found out I had Type-2 diabetes and my cholesterol numbers were through the roof. The doctor told me in no uncertain terms that if I didn't lose weight, I'd likely be dead before I was forty. My father had died at forty from a massive heart attack, so I knew it was a distinct possibility."

"Wow, that's scary!" Beth exclaimed, her eyes wide. "Did you go on a diet?"

"I did. I joined Weight Watchers, learned about portion control and eating healthy foods."

"Did you start going to the gym, too?"

"Not at first. I was too embarrassed. Besides, I couldn't walk up the stairs without getting winded. So I started slow by walking a half a block, then a block, then two. Pretty soon I was running, and when the weight started to come off and I felt more confident, I went to the gym and got myself a trainer. And the rest is history."

"And now you're the trainer," Cara said, "helping

other people lose weight."

Finn shifted his attention to her. "I wanted a whole new life with a whole new career. I went back to school and got certified as a personal trainer. Who better to know what it takes to lose weight than someone who's been there?"

"How much weight did you lose?" Jenna asked.

"One hundred and twenty-eight pounds. Here, I'll show you."

He stood and pulled a large piece of fabric from the shopping bag he'd brought with him. When he held it up, Cara realized it was a massive pair of pants. "I've kept these pants to remind myself that I never want to go back. I know I'll have to watch my weight for the rest of my life, but I swear I'm never going to have to wear these again."

The dark gray fabric could have wrapped around his trim waist at least twice. The magnitude of what he'd accomplished suddenly hit her. He was an amazingly strong and determined person.

"You were huge!" Beth exclaimed.

Finn laughed again. "I certainly was."

"Do you tell your success story to all your wayward clients?" Cara asked, hoping for a light tone. "Does it inspire them to stick to the straight and narrow?"

He sobered. "Actually, I've never told any of my clients this story before. It's private."

"Then why are you telling us?" She held her breath as she waited for his answer.

"Because I don't want you to quit. I want you to know losing weight is possible. And I want you to be happy."

In all the years she'd been married to Peter she couldn't remember him ever being overly concerned about her happiness. What did it mean that Finn was?

"I won't go back to the gym."

"That's okay. I'll come here."

"I don't have workout equipment here."

"Don't need it. We'll walk, and eventually run."

"I don't always have time to shop for fresh fruits and vegetables and cook low-fat meals."

"The girls will help with the cooking, won't you, girls?" His raised eyebrow dared them to contradict him.

"Yeah, for sure, Mom," Jenna said. "We'll help."

She grabbed at straws. "I hate carrots."

He grinned. "You can eat broccoli. Got any more excuses?"

"None that I can think of right now. Give me a minute."

"Nope. Time's up. The program starts tomorrow." Cara couldn't think of a thing to say. As the girls cheered, and Finn filled them in on his plans for her, apprehension niggled at the back of her mind: would being with Finn every day cause her to make a fool of herself over him again?

Chapter Six

The next afternoon at 4:45 Finn showed up at Cara's apartment with two bags of groceries and a stomach full of apprehension. Today would be his first day, again, as Cara's trainer. He straightened his shoulders and lifted his chin, determined she would not get rid of him so easily this time.

He rang the doorbell. He'd rearranged his schedule, fitting clients with different appointments so he could devote this time exclusively to Cara. It occurred to him that he'd practically turned his life upside down for her. He blew out a long breath, not sure what to make of his actions. He'd never gone to so much trouble for a client before. But then, he'd never met anyone like Cara before either.

Did devoting so much time to her mean he was a dedicated professional, or a gigantic fool?

Beth answered the doorbell. "Mom phoned to say she's running late but she should be home in about fifteen minutes."

His heart fell. He hadn't realized how badly he'd wanted to see her. He covered his disappointment with a smile. "That gives us time to get dinner ready. May I come in?"

Beth stepped aside. "Oh, sure. We were just finishing our homework."

"Good, you can help cook dinner."

Both girls followed him into the kitchen. "Hi, Finn. What are we having for supper?" Jenna asked.

He started unpacking the grocery bags. "We're having baked chicken with vegetables and a tossed salad."

"Sounds kind of boring," Beth complained.

"Can we have some fries with that?"

"Losing weight is hard enough, but when the rest of the family is eating fries and ice cream, it's even tougher. Don't you want to help your mom? Getting in shape means a lot to her."

"She wants to look good for her reunion," Jenna said. "I guess it wouldn't kill us to eat vegetables for awhile."

"I want to help Mom," Beth said. "What do you want us to do?"

"How about washing the vegetables and getting the salad ready? For dessert we're having fresh strawberries and yogurt."

"Okay, that doesn't sound too gross," Beth conceded.

Finn grinned. "Glad you approve, because you're going to have to wash the strawberries, too. Come on, let's get started."

While the girls washed the vegetables, Finn deboned and skinned the chicken.

"So what are some of your mom's favorite things to eat?"

"She really likes Doritos," Jenna said.

"I was thinking more about her favorite vegetables and fruits."

"I don't know," Beth said, placing a floret of broccoli in the strainer. "We haven't been eating a lot of fruits and vegetables. Not since we moved here. Mostly we eat frozen dinners."

"Mom's so busy with work and getting us to soccer games that she doesn't have much time to cook," Jenna said as she peeled a carrot. "Before Dad moved out, she used to cook a lot. Mostly fancy things that he liked."

"When Dad moves back home, she won't have to work anymore, so she can cook again."

Finn's heart sank at Beth's words. Was a reconciliation between Cara and her ex imminent?

Jenna gave her sister an exasperated look. "Beth, I've told you a hundred times. They're not getting back together."

He let out the breath he'd been holding, feeling like he was on a roller coaster ride.

"Why do you think Mom wants to lose weight for this reunion? It's so when Dad sees her all pretty and slim again, he'll fall in love with her all over."

"Beth, your mom is beautiful the way she is. She shouldn't have to lose weight so that your Dad loves her again. If you love someone, truly love them, it shouldn't matter what they look like."

Beth stuck her chin out at a defiant angle. "I know Mom still loves Dad. Why would she keep his picture in her room if she didn't?"

Yes, Finn, why would she keep a picture of her ex in her bedroom if she didn't still feel something for him?

"Don't be an idiot. You know Mom is keeping that picture for us. She's told you that."

"I think she wants to keep it for herself," Beth said stubbornly. "I *know* she still loves him."

Jenna rolled her eyes and went back to peeling

carrots. Finn began chopping the washed vegetables. It was inevitable that Cara would still have feelings for the father of her children, the man she'd lived with for twenty years. But was she still in love with him? Was the whole point of losing weight just to get Peter back? Did he have any hope of winning her affections?

Cara didn't talk about Peter as if she were still in love with him. In fact, Finn had the distinct impression he had hurt her a lot. But sometimes feelings of love refused to die.

So where did that leave him?

"Hey, everybody, I'm home. Sorry I'm late. Traffic was murder tonight." Cara breezed into the kitchen with kisses for both girls and a smile for him. "So this is Day One of my new diet?"

Finn smiled back, feeling like a teenager discovering girls for the first time. He stifled the impulse to touch her hair, and run his finger down her silky cheek. "Don't think of it as a diet but as a lifestyle change. Think how fantastic you're going to feel with all this healthy eating."

She sighed. "I know you're right. But can you give me a few moments to mourn? The Doritos and I had a very close relationship."

He loved her sense of humor. "Don't spend too much time in black." He popped a carrot stick in her mouth. "Here. Meet your new best friend."

Cara closed her eyes and bit into the carrot, making a face as she chewed.

"I don't know. Mr. Carrot here is a little on the bland side. I always loved the spicy Latin fire of my old best friend, Mr. Dorito."

"Yeah, but Mr. Dorito will leave you empty and

hurting. Mr. Carrot only has your best interests at heart."

She sighed. "I know you're right, but I still think carrots are boring."

Did she feel the same way about him?

He placed the casserole dish into the preheated oven. "While supper's cooking, let's go for a walk."

A short time later they were heading down the street in a brisk walk. Cara turned to him with a shy smile. "I've got to tell you how much I appreciate you doing this for me. Losing this weight means a lot to me, but I don't think I could do it without you."

Finn gazed into her beautiful hazel eyes and tumbled headfirst into love. He'd fought it as long as he could but it was all over for him now. Cara had totally captured his heart and there was no going back.

But would she always consider him bland Mr. Carrot while pining away for Mr. Dorito, her spicy first love?

****

Three days later, Cara arrived home to delicious cooking smells and her daughters' laughter. Her heart lightened as she listened to the good-natured banter between the girls and Finn coming from the kitchen, and she wondered what Day Four of her new diet held in store. She had to admit that so far Finn's food choices had been surprisingly tasty, and she hadn't yet felt the desire to stray off the path into junk food oblivion.

"Hello, everybody. So what's on the menu today?"

"You're in for a treat," Finn said with a smile. "We've created a new dish, just for you. Tofu and Vegetable Stir-Fry Surprise."

Cara wrinkled her nose in feigned disapproval as she eyed the contents of the wok in Finn's hand. "You're kidding me, right? Tofu? What's the surprise?"

He grinned as he tossed ingredients in the pan. "The surprise is how much you're going to like it. Keep an open mind. Remember, you promised to try new dishes and alternative ways of cooking."

"I don't suppose any of your new dishes involve chocolate bars or cheesecake?"

Finn's laughter sent a ripple of pleasure down Cara's spine. She loved the deep timbre of it and the way his dimples popped out when he smiled. Mostly she loved the fact that she could make him laugh.

"Sorry. The first few weeks of this regime are short on candy and cheesecake, but once you're at the point of maintaining your weight, we'll work in a few treats, in moderation. I don't believe in forbidden foods. If I tell myself I can't have a certain food, it makes me want it more, and I'm more likely to overindulge."

Beth popped a fresh strawberry into her mouth. "We went through all the cupboards, the fridge, and the freezer, and threw out all the junk food."

Cara wondered if they'd found the secret stash of taco chips in her bedroom closet. "Thanks for being so helpful, girls."

"No problem, Mom." Jenna rinsed lettuce under the tap. "Finn's going to take us all shopping tomorrow and teach us how to read labels. Isn't that right, Finn?"

"You bet. How about adding some other vegetables to the salad? The more interesting it is, the less likely we are to be tempted by cheesecake."

When he gave Cara a conspiratorial wink, she couldn't help but smile back. She poured herself a glass of water, then sat at the table. Like he'd been doing it for years, Finn moved around her small kitchen with the grace of an athlete. He was a nice man to come home to. Not only was he cooking dinner for her, he was extremely easy on the eyes. She enjoyed his quick wit and the way he filled her home with laughter. His positive energy rubbed off on all of them. Beth acted less worried, Jenna seemed less angry, and she herself was content, even happy.

That revelation came as a huge surprise. Happiness had been a rare commodity for a long time.

Cara marveled at Finn's patience with the girls, and at their willingness to follow his instructions. She watched as he helped Beth mix oil and lemon juice and spices for the salad dressing, then demonstrated to Jenna the safest way to use a paring knife. They sucked up the information, and the attention, like a couple of thirsty sponges. When was the last time Peter had bothered to show them anything? She'd been the one who'd taught them to tie their shoes and ride a two-wheeled bike. She'd explained the facts of life and answered their wide-eyed questions. She'd even taught them how to kick a soccer ball. Where exactly had their father been in their lives?

The salad was soon tossed and the stir-fry placed in a serving dish and brought to the table. Cara went to the cupboard for dishes to set the table. Finn put his hand on her arm. "Oh, no, you don't. You worked all day. It's our turn to take care of things. Isn't that right, girls?"

"Yeah," Jenna said as she put plates on the table. "Finn says it's our turn to cook for a change."

Beth put cutlery and napkins next to the plates.

"Besides, he promised to take us out for frozen yogurt tomorrow if we helped out."

"Aha! The truth comes out!"

Finn set glasses on the table. "I'm not above using bribery to get what I want."

As promised, the tofu surprise tasted surprisingly delicious. Reveling in the girls' laughter, Cara enjoyed both the meal and the company. They chatted about their day, while she and Finn listened and offered comments. It was good to see them in such high spirits.

It almost felt like the four of them were a family.

"Are you ready for our power walk?" Finn asked her after everyone finished eating.

Cara groaned. "Isn't there some rule about having to wait an hour after eating before exercising?"

"That's only for swimming. Trust me, you'll be fine. Go get changed."

She couldn't put it off any longer. "I'll be right back."

After throwing on a pair of shorts and a T-shirt, she caught her hair into a haphazard ponytail and stepped into the living room. Finn waited for her by the door, looking through some papers she'd left there. He held up a brochure. "I couldn't help seeing this. Are you thinking about trying this?"

Cara's face flushed with embarrassment when she realized what he was holding. "Oh, the zooni berry diet. My ever-helpful mother sent it to me."

"Your mother?"

"She never misses an opportunity to point out my inadequacies. Are you ready to go?"

"Sure." He gave her a couple of hand weights. "These are two and a half pounds each. We'll work your arms while we walk."

Finn set a brisk pace; Cara struggled to keep up and soon her breathing became labored. Her biceps screamed with the effort of pumping the weights.

"Does your mother often send you stuff like that?"

"You mean the brochure? Occasionally, but she usually prefers to dispense her advice in person, or on the phone now that she and my father have moved to Florida." A move for which she thanked God every day.

"It sounds like you don't get along with her."

"It's hard to get along with someone who criticizes everything you do."

"Has she always been like that?"

"Only when I haven't lived up to her high standards. She was very proud of me in high school when I made the cheerleading squad, and served as class president during my junior year." Was pleasing her mother part of the reason she'd worked so hard to be popular back then? "And she loved Peter. Having her daughter marry into the prominent McLeod family was quite a feather in her cap. Of course, she blames me entirely for the breakdown of my marriage."

"I'm sorry you don't have a better relationship with her."

"It's no big deal." But her stomach knotted in pain, contradicting her words and making her wince.

"You okay?"

She managed a smile. "Never better."

"Do you want to take a break?"

"No, let's keep going."

It killed her that he wasn't even winded. But no matter how tired she felt or how miserable thinking about her mother made her, she'd be damned if she'd give up now that she was finally on track. Her pride demanded that if she attended the reunion, she'd go a few pounds lighter and several inches slimmer. She could hardly wait to see the look on Peter's face when she walked into the Summerville Inn.

"You're smiling. What's so funny?"

"Just doing a little visualization exercise."

"Oh, yeah? What were you visualizing?"

"Sweet revenge." Cara laughed, giving her weights an exuberant swing. "I'm thinking about how great it's going to feel to hold my head up with pride when I talk to Peter at the reunion."

His smile disappeared just before he averted his gaze. "It's important to you that he see you as attractive again."

She dragged more oxygen into her lungs and forced her tired arms to keep pumping. "He made it quite clear that my weight was partially to blame for the breakup of our marriage. I'm just tired of feeling so…so blimp-like."

"You, a blimp? Not even close. Take it from someone who's been there."

"I keep forgetting that you were once overweight, too."

"Not just overweight. Obese."

She dared a glance at him. He stared straight ahead, his jaw clenched and his mouth unsmiling.

"What was your life like before you lost weight?" she asked, overtaken by the sudden need to know more about him.

"Lonely."

For a moment Cara thought he would say nothing

more, but then he began to speak. "I didn't have a lot of friends because, quite frankly, I wasn't a lot of fun to be around. Women looked at me either with pity or disgust. I hated my job as a warehouse manager, and I hated being the constant butt of jokes. My stepmother and sister were only interested in watching TV and eating."

Her heart broke at the thought of how miserable he must have been. "You sound like you were so unhappy."

"Yeah. I was."

Cara wondered if she would have been cruel and dismissive toward him if she'd known him back then. "Tell me about your family. What are your stepmother and sister like?"

"What do you want to know?"

"I don't know. Stuff. How old is your sister?"

"Twenty-six. Susie's my half-sister, actually."

"So your stepmother is her mother."

"Yes."

"When did your father marry your stepmother?"

She heard him sigh. "When I was about five. Susie was born when I was nine."

"What was your childhood like?"

The corner of his mouth lifted slightly. "Happy. I don't remember my mother well, but I know that I was loved. She died when I was four."

"I'm sorry. That must have been so hard for you and your dad."

"It was, but I don't remember being scared or unhappy as long as my dad was around. He always made me laugh."

"You said he died when he was forty. How old

were you?"

"About thirteen. For the first time in my life, I felt totally alone."

Cara's heart ached for the boy. "But you still had your stepmother and sister."

"Dad was the glue in our family. Once he was gone, Pauline kind of fell apart and took Susie and me with her. She stopped going out with friends and just stayed home and ate. She'd been overweight before, but then her weight went through the roof. She couldn't handle even small, everyday problems, so I tried to look after her and Susie the best I could. We all ate as if somehow that would bring Dad back. None of us knew any other way of coping with his death."

"Oh, Finn, that's so sad."

He turned to look at her. "I didn't tell you this to make you feel sorry for me."

Actually, she was in awe of his strength. He'd overcome a lot of heartache and hardship to get to the place he was now. "How are they doing these days?"

Finn sighed again. "Pauline just turned sixty, but she looks years older. Her health is lousy because she chain smokes and eats all the wrong foods. Susie still lives with her, which is a mistake. She should be out partying with friends and dating and enjoying her life. Instead she comes home from her office job, parks herself in front of the TV, and doesn't stop eating until she goes to bed. She won't let me help her."

"You can't help someone who doesn't want to be helped."

"No, I guess not." He suddenly laughed. "You know what motivated me the most to lose weight?"

"You mean besides the possibility of having a fatal

heart attack?"

"The health stuff was pretty scary, but what I wanted most of all was a girlfriend."

"Of course. Everyone wants someone to love."

"When I was fat, girls wouldn't look at me, but when I started losing weight, they threw themselves my way. I felt like a kid in a candy store."

Cara quashed an inexplicable feeling of jealousy for all these nameless women. "That must have made you happy."

"It did—for a while. Then I finally realized that whether I was fat or thin, for all of these women it was about how I looked, not who I was. None of them actually saw the real me."

She knew exactly what he meant. She doubted Peter had ever seen past her looks to the person she was inside. And when her looks failed, so did his love.

"Someday you'll find someone who loves you for the great guy you are, and you'll have lots of little ones running around."

"Maybe."

"Don't you want kids?"

He shrugged. "Maybe. If it happens with the right person, great, but I wouldn't marry just to have a family. The marriage and the person I marry is the most important thing."

"You're so great with my girls, it would be a shame if you didn't have kids of your own."

Again, he gave a noncommittal shrug. "It's time to head back," he said. "Are you still okay?"

"Yeah, I'm good." She cleared her throat. "Thank you for telling me about your family. I know it's hard for you to talk about them."

"It's easier with you. Because you're my friend, I guess."

Perhaps it was possible to be Finn's friend. Their age difference ruled out any other kind of relationship, because she couldn't bear the inevitable comments about robbing the cradle.

Did she want something more than friendship from Finn?

She risked a sidelong glance at him. He gave her an encouraging grin, his beautiful smile making her heart tumble in her chest. The man was positively, gloriously gorgeous.

In addition, a funny, kind, sincere, and genuinely nice man was wrapped inside that pretty package. And that was far more appealing than six-pack abs could ever be.

Chapter Seven

For two weeks, the station buzzed with the news that the famous writer Kirby Stevens would be a guest on *Rochester Noon.* After the producers of the show heard the prolific author of horror novels would be in Rochester as part of the launch of his latest book, they were thrilled when he agreed to drop in for an interview. Most of the guests of *Rochester Noon* were local politicians and business people, community organizers, and kids who'd done well at the national spelling bee. Stevens was a real coup.

The day of the big interview finally arrived. Kirby Stevens, a tall, distinguished-looking gentleman in his sixties, arrived at the station at the appointed time, an hour before airtime. Michael D'Angelo, the owner of WBST, met him at reception, along with Bill and Cara. Several employees, fans of his work, hung in the background to get a look at the famous author.

"Welcome to WBST," D'Angelo said, shaking his hand. "We're honored to have you with us." He introduced Bill and Cara. "Our host, Jessica Frampton, should be along momentarily. Cara, why don't you take our guest to the green room and make sure he's comfortable."

"Of course. Mr. Stevens, if you'll come this way, I'll get you settled."

"This is a nice place you've got here," he said as

they walked through the building. "I've been at a lot of TV and radio stations in the last few years, and this is the first one with an atrium in the lobby. It's very nice."

"It is rather nice, isn't it?" She loved coming out to the lobby on breaks, especially on dreary winter days. The two-story glass enclosure greeted guests as they entered the station. Three full-grown trees grew in the atrium, along with a garden of other flowers and plants. Sunny and bright, the area always smelled like spring.

"When I'm not writing, I like to garden, so I notice stuff like that. I find digging in the dirt relaxing and very therapeutic."

"Wasn't the villain in *The House on Bleak Street* a gardener? He whacked his victims on the head with his gardening spade, then buried them under the petunias. That one made me afraid to water my geraniums for weeks."

"You've read my books?"

"Oh, yes. You've given me many sleepless nights, Mr. Stevens."

"That's high praise indeed. And please, call me Kirby."

Cara smiled. "Thank you, Kirby."

They arrived at the green room and she let them in. "The washroom is over there. The fridge is stocked with bottled water, juice, and soft drinks. I just made the coffee, so it's fresh. I've got fruit here, but if you'd like something else, like a pastry or yogurt, I can run down to the cafeteria and get it for you."

"No, this is perfect, thank you. I've got everything I need." He patted the bag he carried. "I've got my laptop with me, so I'll be busy working on revisions."

"I'll leave you to your work, then. I'll be back to

pick you up in about an hour."

"I'll see you then."

Cara closed the green room door, smoothing her new skirt. She'd splurged on a new outfit for this occasion, and had taken extra care with her hair, even opting to wear makeup today. Kind of silly, really. She was sure Kirby hadn't noticed how she was dressed, but it made her feel like a real professional. It had been a long time since she'd bothered much with her appearance.

The best part came when she'd tried on the clothes in the dressing room of the store and discovered she was now *two sizes smaller* then the last time she'd gone shopping. Hallelujah! That put a little spring in her step. Certainly Peter would sit up and pay attention to her at the reunion.

When she reached the set, everyone seemed to be running around in a fluster. Bill mopped sweat from his brow as he came toward her. "Oh, my God. Have you heard?"

"Have I heard what?"

"Jessica had a car accident on the way to the station."

"Oh, no. Is she all right?"

"She's going to be fine, but she's pretty banged up. They're keeping her in the hospital overnight." He shook his head. "Stupid woman. She was reading Kirby Stevens's latest book while she was driving and went right through a red light."

Only Jessica would think that driving and reading went well together. "Well, Kirby's books are pretty hard to put down."

"Apparently she'd never read one before. That's

why she was cramming before the big interview. What are we going to do? We've got one of America's best writers in the green room and no host to interview him."

Despite her dislike of Jessica, Cara didn't wish injury on her, especially when it threw the show into chaos. "What about Tony Monroe? He's subbed for Jessica a few times."

"I've already called him. He's on assignment in Los Angeles. Martha Peary is in Europe, and Michelle Tang is about to give birth any minute. None of our regular subs are available. What are we going to do?"

He mopped his brow again, then cocked his head. "You look very nice today."

"Thank you." They were in the middle of a crisis. Why would Bill suddenly notice her new outfit? "I wanted to spruce up a little, since Kirby Stevens is one of my favorite authors."

"You've read his books?"

"All of them. I'm a huge fan."

His eyes lit up. "I just had a brilliant idea."

Cara didn't like that look. "Oh, no." She backed away. "You're not thinking...oh, no."

"It's perfect, don't you see? You're dressed up, you've read all of Stevens's books. You can interview him!"

"I've never interviewed anyone in my life!"

"Jessica does it all the time. How hard can it be?" He pulled a list of questions from his clipboard. "Here. This is her script with the prepared questions since she rarely has one of her own."

Suddenly, her stomach threatened to dislodge the whole-grain cereal she'd eaten that morning. "Being on camera is nerve-racking. I don't know if I can handle it."

"Cara, as a friend, I can tell you your talents are wasted as a junior assistant. You're way too smart to be serving coffee to guests. And as your boss, I'm telling you that I need you to step in and do this job." He grasped her shoulder. "I wouldn't ask if I didn't think you could handle it."

"You're not just saying that because your butt's on the line?"

He nodded. "My butt may be on the line, but I really think you can do it."

Cara opened her mouth to speak, but nothing came out. Nancy's words came back to her: *What do you have to do to not feel like a failure?*

Perhaps proving to herself that she could handle this situation would be a step toward regaining her confidence. *But did it have to be such a scary step?* She took a deep breath. "Okay. I'll do it, but remember, this was your idea."

Bill winked at her. "Best one I've had all day."

He hurried away to let the rest of the crew know about the change. Cara wiped her suddenly sweaty palms on her new skirt. Good lord, what had she gotten herself into?

****

Kate hurried toward Finn in the middle of the gym. "There's a phone call for you. She says it's urgent."

"Who is it?" He was in the middle of a training session. His stepmother had called more than once with an "urgent" message that turned out to be a plugged drain or a broken television.

"Cara McLeod."

Cara had never called him at work, and he knew she wouldn't unless it was extremely important. Had she been in an accident? Were one of the girls injured?

"Tom, I've got to take this," he told his client. "Why don't you take a five-minute break? Kate, can you send the call to my office?"

"Will do."

Weaving between machines and dodging customers, he raced into his office. By the time he reached his desk, fear and exertion had him in a lather. He grabbed the phone. "Cara? Sweetheart, are you okay?"

"Yes, I'm fine. I'm...oh, my God, Finn. I'm scared to death."

His gut twisted. "What's wrong?"

"I'm going to interview Kirby Stevens, on live television!" She told him the story of Jessica's accident, and the instant, though temporary, promotion. "I'm scared. What if I mess up?"

"Take a deep breath and think. Realistically, what's the worst thing that could happen?"

"I make a bloody fool of myself and drool all over my favorite author."

"Cara, I said realistically."

"Okay, okay." She paused, and Finn could practically hear the wheels turning in her head. "What scares me most is that this interview is scheduled for the full hour of the show. I'm afraid that somewhere around the halfway mark, I'll run out of things to say, and we'll have dead air for thirty minutes."

A legitimate concern, he thought. "When I was a guest, Jessica had a list of questions for me. Do you have something like that?"

"Yes. Bill prepared questions for this interview, too."

"Good, good. Do you know anything about this writer?"

"I don't know anything about his personal life, but I've read all his books. He's an amazing writer."

"Perfect. Ask him about his books. People love to talk about themselves. My suggestion is to study all the questions so you're ready if you run out of things to say, but just be yourself. You're warm and funny and you put people at ease. People like talking to you."

There was a pause on the line and for a moment Finn thought the phone had gone dead. Then he heard Cara's whispered reply. "Thanks, Finn. I'm glad I called you. I feel so much better." Another pause. "Oh, my gosh. I must have taken you away from work. I'm sorry."

"Not a problem. I'm sure Tom is glad for the break." He chuckled. "Jessica better watch her back. You could give her a run for her money."

Cara's throaty laugh made various parts of his anatomy tingle in response. "Yes, that's my evil plan. Take over *Rochester Noon*, then the world."

"If you set your mind to it, I'm sure you could do it."

"Thanks, Finn."

"For what?"

"Believing in me."

"Are you going to be okay now?"

"I'm fine. Thanks to you."

He wanted so badly to tell her he loved her, adored her, thought she was the most amazing woman in the world. Fear stopped him. Was she truly over her ex-husband? Why else would losing weight for the reunion be so important to her if not to impress Peter?

"I've got to run," she said. "Thanks again. I'll talk to you later at my condo, right?"

"Absolutely. I can hardly wait to hear about your big TV debut. Break a leg. Isn't that what they say in show biz?"

She laughed. "Yeah, that's what they say. Bye."

Finn replaced the receiver and closed his eyes. *Why doesn't she realize how amazing she is?*

Then again, if she did would there still be room in her life for him?

****

"You mentioned earlier that you're working on a new novel. Can you tell us a little about it?"

"Sure. It's about a mysterious virus that infects the inhabitants of a small North Dakota town after a nearby Sioux burial ground is unearthed to make room for a golf course. Every seven days, the people of Paradise, North Dakota, experience fevered hallucinations in which they are thrust back in time and become the ancient Sioux whose bones were disturbed."

"Sounds exciting. Do they all experience the same hallucination together?"

"They do. It's an alternate dimension, except in this dimension friends are now enemies, and unlikely couples in the modern world are now passionate lovers. When they're awake, they are able to recall everything that happened during their dream state. Except to them, it feels more real than real life."

"Will they eventually stay in the ancient world?"

Kirby offered Cara an enigmatic smile. "Perhaps, perhaps not."

"Is that all you're going to tell me?"

"I'm afraid so. I have to leave some mystery for the readers."

"I can hardly wait to read this one. What do you call it?"

"*Paradise Lost.*"

"Great title. I'll be sure to watch for it."

Cara blinked as Bill signaled the two-minute warning. She couldn't believe how quickly the hour had flown by. Interviewing Kirby Stevens had been amazingly easy. He was interesting, funny, and erudite. She'd started out by asking him about his books, and his writing schedule, and he took it from there. Like Finn said, most people loved talking about themselves, and the famous author was no exception.

After signing off, Cara extended a hand to him. "Thank you so much for making my first television interview such a pleasure. You were a wonderful guest."

"You're a natural, Cara. It was my pleasure to be your first interviewee. I'm sure I won't be your last."

"Oh, no, I was just pinch-hitting for Jessica. I'm pretty much a one-hit wonder."

Michael D'Angelo joined them. "Don't be so sure of that, Cara. Mr. Stevens, thank you again for being our guest."

Kirby shook D'Angelo's hand. "I enjoyed it immensely. It's wonderful to be interviewed by someone who's actually read my books. That doesn't always happen."

"Let me walk you to the green room to retrieve your things," Cara said. "I know you have to get to another interview this afternoon."

"I'm sure it won't be as much fun as this one."

"Cara, can I see you in my office once Mr. Stevens is on his way?"

She blinked. What could the station owner possibly want with her? "Yes, of course."

D'Angelo turned his attention to their guest. "I hope you'll drop by again the next time you're in Rochester."

Kirby smiled. "I certainly will. Thank you."

Cara and Kirby walked to the green room to pick up his laptop before heading to the front door, where a car sent by his publisher was waiting for him. He took her hand. "Wonderful meeting you. Best of luck."

"Thank you. It was a thrill to meet you. Good luck with *Paradise Lost*."

"I'll be sure to send you a copy."

Touched, Cara said, "I'd love that."

She waved goodbye as he drove off, then took a deep breath. Mr. D'Angelo was waiting for her.

She'd never been on the third floor of the TV station where all the executives had their posh offices. She wandered about, a little lost, until she found a friendly secretary who pointed the way to the owner's office. She found the door, wiped her damp palms on her skirt, and knocked.

"Come in," D'Angelo boomed from the other side.

"You wanted to see me?" she said as she stood on the threshold.

"Please, close the door and come in and sit down."

Cara sat in one of the chairs in front of the desk and folded her hands in her lap. Mr. D'Angelo took the seat next to her. "I guess you're wondering why I asked you here."

"I'm really hoping it's not to fire me."

He flashed a disarming grin. "No, not at all. In fact, I want to offer you a promotion."

"A promotion? Really?" Dollar signs flashed in her head. If she made more money she wouldn't have to depend so much on Peter's payments.

"I was very impressed with you today. Your interview skills are first rate. Have you worked in journalism before?"

"Not really, unless you count my stint as an ace reporter on my high school paper."

"I don't think I'd put it on my resume if I were you," he said, grinning. "You have a natural ability to make people comfortable during an interview. You gave Mr. Stevens your complete attention, and I'm sure he felt that way, as well. And even though you filled in for Jessica at the last minute, you appeared well prepared."

"It was easy with Mr. Stevens. I've been a fan of his for years, and I love his work."

"Would you be interested in becoming the host of *Rochester Noon*?"

Cara stared at him. Had she just stepped into an alternate dimension of her own?

Chapter Eight

When Cara breezed into the condo late that afternoon, the radiant smile on her face and excitement in her eyes told Finn something had changed. She looked more beautiful than ever.

Eyes dancing, she took a seat at the kitchen table. "I've been offered the job as host of *Rochester Noon*!"

"You mean permanently?" Finn asked. "Not just the one time?"

"Yes! They actually want me to host the show on a permanent basis!" She squeezed Jenna's hand. "Your mother, the TV star."

She told the girls how she'd stepped in to interview Kirby Stevens after Jessica's accident. "So Mr. D'Angelo said he liked my interview skills. Actually, he said I had a lot of warmth and personality and that the viewing audience would respond to that. Can you believe it?"

"I can totally believe it," Finn said. Her kindness, humility, and genuine interest in people would keep people glued to their sets. "You're going to be a great host, Cara, but I've got to ask, what happened to Jessica? Was she hurt that badly in the accident?"

"No, she's going to be fine, just a lot of bumps and bruises. It turns out Mr. D'Angelo has wanted to replace her for a while because of lousy ratings. Jessica's abrasive style turns off a lot of viewers. He was waiting to find the right person."

"And now he has," Finn said. "How did she take the news?"

She winced. "Not well. Bill said when he and Mr. D'Angelo went to the hospital to tell her she wasn't coming back to WBST, she threw a hissy fit, then chucked a plastic water jug at the boss's head."

"I hope she doesn't expect to get a good reference."

"I'm not sure which upset her more: being replaced, or being replaced by the oldest junior assistant at the station. I feel kind of sorry for her."

"Don't worry about Jessica," Finn said. "I have a feeling she's going to land on her feet."

Cara grinned. "The rumor around WBST is that a TV station in Los Angeles is looking to hire her as their weather girl. I'm sure Jessica will tell everyone that leaving *Rochester Noon* was her idea."

"Will this mean you'll be making more money?" Jenna asked.

"Yes, it definitely does!"

"Cool. Congratulations, Mom."

"Thanks, honey."

"Mom, with this new job, we won't be moving or anything, will we?" Beth asked, a worried frown on her face. Finn knew her well enough by now to understand she didn't adapt easily to change. She'd had plenty of upheaval in her young life and wasn't anxious for more.

Cara stroked her hair. "No, honey. I'll be working for the same TV station, in the same building, just a different job. There's no moving involved."

Beth threw her arms around Cara's neck. "In that case, congratulations, Mom. You're so smart."

She held her tight. "Thank you, baby. That's the nicest thing anyone's ever said to me."

She kissed Beth's forehead before letting her go. The girls resumed washing and dicing vegetables for a salad. Cara looked up at Finn. "I couldn't have gone on the air today without speaking to you first. Thanks for the pep talk."

"You're welcome. I knew you could do it. Congratulations, Cara."

He leaned in close, going for a congratulatory peck. But when his lips touched her soft, sweet mouth, his rational brain stopped functioning and his body took over. He pulled her close, molding her against his chest. She stiffened for one moment before relaxing and sighing against his mouth. Warmth enveloped him as she wound her arms around his neck. Finn lost himself in her intoxicating scent and the feel of her in his arms.

"Mom!"

Beth's indignant cry broke through to Finn's sex-addled brain. Cara jerked away from him as if she'd been scalded, her eyes wide. They stared at each other until she gathered her wits and asked, "What's for dinner? I'm starved."

"Stir fry with vegetables and beef," Jenna said, giving Finn a wink.

"I'm tired of vegetables," Beth said, setting down her knife. "I want a hot dog."

"We don't have hot dogs, sweetie," Cara said, smoothing her youngest daughter's long, straight hair. "You guys threw out all the junk food, remember? Besides, stir fry sounds good."

Beth threw the bell pepper she'd been slicing to the floor. "I don't want any stupid stir fry." Then she aimed a deadly look at Cara. "Why did you kiss him like that?"

"Finn was simply congratulating me, honey. It didn't mean anything."

Her words cut him to the quick. A kiss that meant everything to him meant nothing to her.

Beth ran from the kitchen. Her bedroom door slammed shut, the sound reverberating through the condo. The look of utter devastation on Cara's face tore at Finn's heart.

"I'll go talk to her," he said.

"No, I think it might be better if I talk to her. Maybe you should leave."

She's sending me away. Anxiety settled in a lump in the pit of his stomach. "What about your exercise for tonight? We were going to try to intersperse a little running between the walks."

"I'll walk by myself tonight." She held up her hand when he tried to argue. "I'll be fine."

"All right." Not wanting to leave, Finn reluctantly slipped on his jacket. "I'll see you tomorrow then?"

She gave him a vague nod. "Goodnight."

He shut the door softly as he left the condo. Would she end their relationship before it had a chance to really begin?

He hated that Beth was upset, especially since it meant that Cara was also upset. Beth believed he stood in the way of her parents' reconciliation. Was she right? Was Cara's reconciliation with her ex imminent?

Where did that leave him?

He knew the answer. Alone.

****

Cara knocked softly on her daughter's bedroom

door, and waited for Beth's "Come in" before entering. As she sprawled face down on the twin bed, Beth's blonde hair fanned out on the comforter, her long coltish legs hanging over the edge. Cara's heart constricted. Physically, her little girl was no longer a baby. In the last year, she'd shot up in height, making her tower over both Cara and her sister. But despite her maturing body, Beth was still just thirteen, caught somewhere between childhood and womanhood.

Cara sat next to her and stroked her hair. "I'm sorry you're upset."

"Why did you have to kiss Finn like that? It was gross."

It was anything but gross. "It was just a kiss, Beth. Finn and I are friends. Like I said, he was congratulating me, that's all."

Beth turned to look at her and pushed her hair out of her eyes. "It didn't look like a *friend* kiss to me. More like a boyfriend kiss."

It felt like a boyfriend kiss, too. "Well, it wasn't."

"Don't you miss Daddy even a little bit?"

Cara hesitated before answering. She missed being part of a couple, and she missed having her family intact. She missed a strong male body holding her in the night, and she definitely missed sex. But did she miss Peter? "Honey, your dad and I were unhappy together. Sometimes married people grow apart and everyone is happier living in separate houses."

"I'm not happier. I miss him."

"I know you do."

Though Peter had been generous financially in providing the girls with whatever they needed for school or soccer, he'd been less generous with his time.

He never came to any of their games, though Cara had sent him the schedules. In the past three years he'd shown up twice for school events. The girls stayed with him only once every six to eight weeks—by his choice. He loved them, but on his own terms, and had no interest in day-to-day parenting. It hurt to see Beth suffer because of his indifference.

"Do you think you and Daddy will ever get back together again?"

"Beth"—Cara sighed—"you've asked me this before and I've always told you no. Your dad has moved on with his life."

"Have you moved on, too?"

The question stopped her cold. Had she moved on? Or was some part of her unconsciously waiting for Peter to change his mind and come back?

She didn't want to give Beth any reason to hang on to false hope, even though she wasn't sure it was the truth. "Yes, I've moved on. Now, come out into the kitchen and have dinner with Jenna and me."

"Isn't Finn here?"

"No, he went home."

Beth sat up. "I'm sorry, Mom. I like him."

"I know you do, and I know he likes you too. Come on. Let's go have dinner. I'm starved."

Beth got to her feet and Cara put her arm around her shoulders as they walked to the kitchen. But she couldn't get her daughter's question out of her head.

Have you moved on?

She had no idea.

****

Later, while Jenna's team played their cross-town rivals on one field and Beth's team practiced on an adjacent field, Cara took her hand weights from the car in preparation for her power walk. She wished Finn was beside her, encouraging her as he always did. She wondered for the hundredth time why he sacrificed his time to help her. Whatever his reasons, she missed him.

Across the parking lot, Nancy waved before stepping over to Cara's car. "I didn't expect to see you tonight. I thought you'd be with Finn."

So did I. "I'm on my own tonight. Want to join me for my walk?"

Nancy laughed. "I'll give it a shot. I hope I can keep up with you."

They started down a leafy street in the quiet suburban neighborhood surrounding the soccer complex. Cara pumped her arms in time with her legs, making sure to remember to breathe deeply as she did so. Nancy gamely kept pace, doing a combination of running and walking.

"How come I can barely breathe and you're not even winded?" Nancy muttered.

Cara hadn't realized until that moment how strong and in control she felt. Energy soared through her veins. She felt like she could walk for miles. "I guess it's because I've been working so hard the last four weeks. I've got more energy than I've had in years."

She knew she had Finn to thank for that. Without his persistence and patience, she'd still be wallowing in self-pity.

"You look great. How much weight have you lost?"

"I don't know exactly. Finn won't let me check until next week. But all my old clothes are loose, and I'm fitting into smaller skirts these days."

"Clothes don't lie, girlfriend. Congratulations. You've worked really hard."

"Thanks, but I don't think I could have done it without Finn's help."

"You two have been joined at the hip for the last few weeks. Why isn't he here with you tonight, really?"

Cara sighed and told her about her new job and Beth's meltdown, and the conversation she'd had with her daughter. "Ever since Beth asked, I've been trying to figure out if I've really moved on since the divorce—or have I been waiting for Peter to come back?"

"If you are, I think you're going to be headed for more heartache."

"Things weren't good the last few years of my marriage. I tried so hard to be everything Peter wanted, but I was never good enough. Maybe I'm still trying."

Was this why she continued to work so hard to lose weight? So that Peter would fall at her feet at the reunion and tell her how sorry he was?

"You deserve someone who thinks you're pretty terrific just the way you are." Nancy wiped sweat from her brow with her sleeve. "Maybe Finn's that person."

"He's a great guy, but there could never be anything between us."

"Why not?"

"Because he's eight years younger than me, for a start."

"So?"

"So he told me he'd maybe like kids of his own some day, if he finds the right woman."

"Maybe you're the right woman."

"I'm forty-three years old. The biological clock may still be ticking, but the sound is kind of faint."

"Just humor me for a minute. If you were given the green light to have another child, how would you feel about it?"

"I don't know," Cara answered truthfully.

Ten years ago she'd begged Peter for another child. She'd wanted a big family with lots of children. But he'd adamantly refused. Now, things were different. She was forty-three, and her children were teenagers. Maybe she was too old to have another child. Besides, she'd just begun an amazing new career. How could she give that up?

Still, the thought of a baby, Finn's baby, spoke to an emotion deep in her woman's heart.

Puffing, Nancy asked, "Do you like this guy?"

"Yes, of course. I like him very much."

"Are you in love with him?"

The question halted Cara in her tracks. She abruptly stopped walking to stare at her friend, heart racing in fear. "No! No way! Of course not! I can't be in love with him!"

"Why not?"

"I don't want to be in love with anyone. I don't think I could survive another breakup."

"Why would you automatically assume if you entered into a relationship with Finn it would end in a bitter breakup?"

"Don't all relationships end that way?"

Nancy shook her head. "That's a very pessimistic attitude. Don't you believe in love anymore?"

"Love beat me down, broke my heart, and destroyed my confidence. I'm not likely to make the same mistake again."

"Does that mean you've given up on sex, too?"

"I didn't say that. I'm not ready to take a vow of celibacy just yet."

"So you're going to turn into a slut and sleep around with random men just to scratch your itch?"

Cara swatted her friend's arm. "Very funny."

"Seriously, you don't have to be in love with a guy to sleep with him."

"I know. I've just never done anything like that before. I'm not sure I'm hardwired that way."

She'd slept with exactly one man in her life, Peter, and had been madly in love when she'd fallen into bed with him. Was it possible to experience passion without the rest of the package?

"I'm sorry you're so down on love." Nancy put her arm around her shoulder. "I prefer to believe there's someone out there for me. I think taking a chance on love is worth the risk."

Cara almost wished she had Nancy's optimistic heart. "I'll be there to pick up the pieces when your heart gets broken. Again."

"You're such a comfort to me. Can we go back now? I'm exhausted."

"Sure." *Love is worth the risk?* The thought made her shudder.

But she didn't like the idea of sleeping single in a double bed for the rest of her life, either.

****

"It's not much farther, Cara. You can do it!"

Cara ran alongside Finn, breathing hard, but keeping up. Now she remembered why she'd loved running in high school. She liked feeling totally attuned to her body. She could visualize oxygen entering her body and flowing to her heart, her lungs, her legs.

Though it wasn't as effortless as it had been back then, the sense of freedom still made her feel like nothing could stand in her way.

When they came to a stop in front of her condo, Cara bent over with her hands on her thighs to catch her breath. "That was incredible!" she said between gasping breaths. "My first run in twenty-five years. I didn't think I could do it anymore."

"I believe you can do anything you set your mind to. You're an amazing woman."

Finn's unshakeable belief in her was truly humbling. She straightened to look into his eyes. "I don't know why you have so much faith in me, but thank you."

He reached out his hand and gently traced the contours of her cheek. "It's easy to have faith in you, sweetheart."

He lowered his face, his lips touching hers with inexorable sweetness. Cara could have cried, or maybe sung, with joy. She loved the way he tasted, the way he held her, even the way he smelled. She wanted to bury her face in his neck and drink in the sweaty, male scent of him. She wanted to go on tasting him, holding him, touching him forever.

She broke the kiss abruptly, frightened by her thoughts. What was she doing? The last time she checked she was still eight years older than him.

Old enough to know better. What would people say? Would they think she was ridiculous for pursuing a younger man? Good lord, what would her mother say?

"What's wrong?"

"Nothing. Nothing's wrong. I just don't want the

girls to look out the window and see us necking on the front step like a couple of teenagers."

"I'm sure it wouldn't scar them for life."

She stepped back, needing some breathing room. "Beth is still upset about seeing us kiss yesterday. Besides, I need to set a good example for them. I'm the mother of teenage daughters, for heaven's sake."

"So necking on the front steps is bad?"

No, it was really, really good. "Yes, bad."

He stepped forward, closing the distance between them once more. "What are your feelings about necking in the car? Front seat good, backseat bad?"

Visions of them steaming up the windows of her old Honda raced through her head. "Both bad. Very bad."

Finn cupped her chin, then snaked an arm around her waist. Her heart rate quickened at the gleam of passion in his eyes. This was a side of him she'd never seen before and it excited her. "What about necking in your bedroom, lights turned low, soft music playing?"

Temptation nipped at her heels. It would be so easy to lean forward and indulge in another of Finn's intoxicating kisses. And it would be so easy to say yes to sex with him. They were both adults; why shouldn't they enjoy each other?

And think of all the calories a couple of rounds of mind-blowing sex would use.

But fear trumped passion. The idea of baring both her body and her soul to him was more than she could handle right now. He'd probably slept with dozens of beautiful women, much slimmer and younger than she. How did she compete with that?

She put a hand on his chest. "I'm not saying no, not

exactly. It's been a while for me. I just need some time…to think things through."

And to lose ten more pounds.

"It's a big deal for me, too. When we make love, I want you to be sure. I want it to be right for both of us." He locked his arms around her waist, and nibbled at her ear. "I'll be waiting for you."

Cara shivered in response. She hoped she could get past her fears and give herself to Finn.

And when she did, she hoped she didn't disappoint him.

Chapter Nine

Facing the camera, Cara waited for Bill's signal before slapping on a smile for the at-home audience. Butterflies danced a samba in her stomach. Today's topic hit just a little too close to home. From now on, she'd have to screen guests more closely.

"Welcome to *Rochester Noon.* I'm your host, Cara McLeod. With me today is relationship expert Dr. Nadia Cummings, who has just written a book entitled *Beyond Cougars and Sugar Daddies: Why Age Doesn't Matter.* Thank you for being with us today, Dr. Cummings."

The statuesque redhead inclined her head. "Thank you for inviting me."

"Dr. Cummings, in your book, you maintain an age difference between marriage partners is irrelevant. Why is that?"

"There are many reasons for a marriage not to work," the guest responded with practiced ease. "Age doesn't have to be one of them."

Cara stared at her, dumbfounded. The doctor didn't know what the hell she was talking about. "But don't couples separated by a wide age gap face problems that couples of the same age don't have to consider?"

Raising one brow, Cummings sat back in her chair. "What sort of problems?"

"Like whether to have a child, for instance. The

older partner could be collecting a pension by the time the child graduates from high school. People will always assume this person is the kid's grandparent. And if it's the woman who's older, conceiving a child may not even be possible. Then what do they do?"

"There are other options, adoption or surrogacy, for example. The more important question to ask is whether both partners truly want a child, just the same as a couple of the same age should ask themselves."

"What about life goals? An older partner might be in a different place in her life than the younger partner."

"True," Dr. Cummings conceded. "The couple should ask themselves if they're a good fit for each other. Does your partner 'seem' like the same age? Do they share some of the same hobbies and interests? There has to be something holding you and your partner together aside from the physical aspects of the relationship. The same holds true for any couple."

Cara wanted to scream. Her *expert* didn't have a clue. She set aside the scripted questions and leaned forward. "But a couple of the same age won't have people whispering behind their backs, saying 'What does he see in that old broad?' They don't have to defend their relationship to anyone. They won't have to worry what anyone thinks."

Cummings cocked her head. "Why do the opinions of others matter to you?"

Cara's face flamed with embarrassment. "I was speaking hypothetically, of course."

"Of course. Well, speaking hypothetically, if the couple is truly happy together, if they have the same goals for family, and they share some of the same interests, what does it matter what anyone else thinks?"

"Perhaps the older partner doesn't want to be thought of as a joke, someone so desperate for love that she needs to rob the cradle. Speaking hypothetically, of course."

"Then I would suggest to this hypothetical older partner that she needs to examine the reasons why she feels so insecure, or she may be losing out on a remarkable relationship with this younger man."

Bill signaled the end of the segment, and Cara hastily said goodbye to her guest before going to commercial. Once they were off the air, Dr. Cummings turned to her with a smile. "If you really care about this man, don't let the opinions of others or your own insecurity keep you apart," she said softly. "Good luck."

Cara watched the doctor leave the set. Did the age thing really matter that much? Was her insecurity causing her to dismiss a potentially wonderful relationship with Finn?

No. She wasn't looking for a marriage partner of any age. She wasn't even looking for a date on Saturday night. She was simply considering Finn as a sexual partner. A friend with benefits, so to speak.

No commitments, no sticky emotions. It was only when love and marriage entered the equation that things got complicated. If nobody said the L-word, nobody got hurt.

It was a good thing she and Finn didn't feel that way about each other.

****

The phone rang just as Finn entered the kitchen at Cara's condo. After Jenna picked it up, her face immediately lost its smile and her body tensed. "Hi,

Grandma. Yes, Beth and I are very well, thank you. How are you and Grandpa?" She began to wave madly at Cara. "I'm sorry to hear that. I hope you feel better soon. Here's my Mom. 'Bye, Grandma."

Jenna thrust the phone into her mother's hand as if she couldn't get rid of it fast enough. Finn's heart broke as Cara took a deep breath before raising the receiver to her ear. "Hi, Mom."

She closed her eyes and rubbed her temple. "Yes, I got your information about the diet. No, I haven't picked up any from the health food store." Wincing, she turned her back to him and after a moment said, "I have my diet under control. We're eating healthy food and— No, I don't want to talk to Alma Lewis's daughter-in-law. I don't even know her. No, I don't think I'm being unreasonable…"

The conversation went on for some time, with Cara defending herself and looking more stressed by the minute. Finally, she waved at Jenna who, taking the obvious cue, dashed to the door and rang the bell.

"Sorry, Mom, I must go. Someone's at the door. 'Bye." She hit the off button and dropped onto a kitchen chair, her whole body sagging in exhaustion.

Finn massaged her shoulders, not knowing what else to do to give her comfort. His stepmother could be difficult, but even at his heaviest, she'd never belittled him the way Cara's mother obviously did her. What kind of woman took pleasure in making her daughter so unhappy?

"Was it a bad one, Mom?" Jenna asked.

"No worse than usual. Thanks for ringing the bell. I needed a reprieve." She moaned and let her head drop forward. "That feels good. You have wonderful hands,

Finn."

His jaw clenched, and he did his best to gentle his hands. She shouldn't have to live this way. "Try to relax. You're all knotted up."

"She always gets that way after Grandma calls," Beth said.

Finn made a decision. "Come on. Let's go for a walk. Just a nice relaxing stroll. And after that, all four of us will go out for frozen yogurt. My treat. How does that sound?"

"Like you're feeling sorry for me," Cara said. "Since I'm already feeling sorry for myself, I'm okay with it." She got to her feet. "Maybe a little exercise will clear my head."

"Good girl."

As they made their way down the sidewalk, he took her hand, wishing he could do something to make things better. "What did your mother say to upset you?"

"The usual. I'm not thin enough, smart enough, good enough. Sometimes it's hard not to believe it."

He put his arm around her waist and kissed her hair. "The rest of the world, including me, thinks you're a beautiful, amazing woman." He paused for a moment. "Have you ever confronted her, told her how hurtful the things she says are? Maybe she'd back off if you told her to mind her own business."

"I've tried, but it doesn't seem to sink in. A counselor once told me that sometimes the only thing to do with a toxic person was to cut them out of your life." She closed her eyes, her expression bleak. "I just haven't found the strength to go that far."

"You're stronger than you think. You can do anything you set your mind to."

She took a deep breath and tried to smile. "I hope you're right."

"I am. Believe it."

Cara squeezed his hand. "Thank you. You're a good friend."

He nodded. Would she ever see him as anything other than a friend?

****

The next afternoon while he was working with a client at the gym, Kate appeared beside him. "There's someone here to see you, Finn."

He looked past the receptionist to see Cara's daughter standing behind her. "Beth? What are you doing here?"

She lowered her gaze, not looking him in the face. "I was hoping I could catch a ride to my house with you."

He turned to his client, who was doing bicep curls with five-pound weights. "Jenny, can you excuse me for a moment? Ten more curls on each arm. I'll be right back."

Finn led Beth toward the waiting area by the front desk. Why had Beth trekked across town to his gym, only to want a ride home again? "I can give you a ride home as soon as I'm finished. How did you get here?"

"I took the bus. And then I walked."

"I see." Beth's face was flushed from the heat, her hair falling out of her ponytail. But beyond that she seemed upset, dispirited even. What on earth had happened? "Wait here for me. I should be done in about fifteen minutes."

He was about to leave when he had a sudden thought. "Does your mother know you're here?"

She lifted her chin in a gesture that reminded him so much of Cara he almost smiled. "I didn't tell her where I was going."

"She's probably home by now and wondering where you are. Come on. Let's give her a call."

He brought her to the front desk and asked Kate to dial Cara's number. Kate handed Beth the phone. "Mom? It's me. I'm at Finn's gym. I know. I'm sorry." She handed the phone to him. "She wants to talk to you."

"Cara, it's Finn."

"Oh, God, I've been frantic. Beth told Jenna she was walking to her friend's house, but when I called she hadn't arrived. Her friend didn't even know she was planning to come. Is she okay?"

"Yes, she's fine. I'll bring her home as soon as I can."

"Okay. What's going on with her? Why would she just take off without telling me?"

"I don't know. I'll see you later."

"Thanks for being there for her."

He disengaged the call and gave the phone back to Kate. "Can you get Beth a bottle of water, please? And you, young lady," he said, turning to Cara's daughter, "stay here until I'm ready to go. Don't get any sudden urges to wander off."

Finn hurried his client through her cool-down routine, and twenty minutes later he and Beth left the gym.

"I thought you had a cell phone," he said as he backed out of his parking spot. "Why didn't you call your mom?"

She sniffed. "I forgot to charge it, so it died."

"My gym is a long way from your house. How did you end up here?"

Beth pulled the elastic from her ponytail, her long hair falling in front of her face and hiding her expression. "Your gym's not far from my dad's office. He's a dentist."

Now we're getting somewhere. "So you came downtown to see your dad."

"Yeah."

"Why didn't you ask him for a ride home?"

She looked out the side window. "Because he was busy."

Too busy to make sure she got safely home? "Did he have an office full of patients?"

"No. He was done for the day." She continued to stare out the side window, voice subdued. "He was on his way to the marina."

"The marina?"

"His friend has a boat. He's taking my dad and a bunch of other people out on the lake for a couple of days. Dad didn't want to be late and disappoint his friend."

But it was okay to disappoint his daughter. "Why didn't you take the bus home instead of coming to my gym?"

"I only had enough money for the one-way fare. I thought Dad would drive me home. Instead, he gave me money for a cab and told me to ask his receptionist to call one for me."

If she'd been his kid, he would have driven her home himself, made sure she was safe. But at least the bastard had given her money. "So why didn't you call the cab?"

She lowered her head and stared at her hands in her lap. "I wanted to see you. To talk, you know?"

He didn't know what to say. He was glad that Beth felt she could come to him with a problem, but damn, she was thirteen years old. Anything could have happened to her while she was on her own.

"Are you mad at me?"

He took a deep breath to calm himself. "I'm not mad that you came to find me. I'm glad you did. But you can't just take off and not tell anyone where you are. It's not safe."

"I know. I'm sorry. I really wanted to see my dad." She folded her hair behind her ear and ventured a look at him. "I wanted to know for sure if he was ever coming back to live with us."

Finn swallowed. "What did he say?"

"He said he liked his life the way it was now, and that he didn't love Mom anymore."

Thank God. "I'm sorry, Beth."

"I asked if I could come live with him. He said no to that, too." Her bottom lip quivered. "He said he loved me, but he was very busy and I was better off living with my mom."

Cara would be crushed to hear this. "Are you that unhappy living with your mom?"

"No." Tears streamed down her face. "I didn't really want to live with Dad. I just wanted to know that I could."

"I'm sorry, Beth." Finn found a package of tissues in the center console and handed it to her. What the hell was he supposed to say to her? Sorry your dad doesn't want you? Too bad he's such a self-centered ass? "We'll be home in a few minutes and everything will be okay."

"You can't tell Mom that I asked Dad if I could live with him. She'd be upset."

"I don't want to keep secrets from your mom."

"Please, Finn."

Damn. He never could say no to a crying female. "Okay, but you have to tell her everything else."

She wiped her eyes and gave him a watery smile. "Thanks. I wanted to see you because I wanted to ask you a question, too."

"It must have been very important for you to come all the way downtown."

"It is. Do you love my mom?"

Finn's heart stopped beating for a moment. This was the last thing he thought she'd ask him. He risked a glance at her. She was watching him intently, body tense as if bracing for bad news. The thing was, he had no idea what she would consider bad news. All he could do was tell the truth. "Yes, I'm in love with your mother."

"You won't be mean to her and make her cry, will you?"

"I never want to make your mom cry."

"Do you want to marry her?"

He hadn't allowed himself to think that far ahead. But now that he'd been asked the question, even if it was by Cara's thirteen-year-old daughter, he knew a life with her was what he wanted. "Yes, I want to marry her, if she'll have me. That's a pretty big if."

The tension left Beth's face. Her smile reminded him of Cara's: pure sunshine. "Thanks for telling me."

"You can't tell her about this conversation, Beth."

Her smile disappeared. "Why not?"

"Because your mother doesn't feel the same way about me, at least not yet. Maybe she never will. But if she does decide to one day fall in love with me, I want it to be her own decision. I don't want her to feel pressured into anything by me or you. Do you understand?"

He heard her sigh. "So, I keep a secret for you and you keep a secret for me?"

"Something like that."

"Okay, I can do that." Another sigh. "Do you think my mom's going to be mad at me?"

"I think that's a safe bet."

"Do you think she's going to ground me?"

He grinned. "Oh, yeah."

****

"You're grounded, young lady!"

When Beth walked through the door with Finn, Cara didn't know whether to kiss her or throttle her. Right after she punished her wayward daughter, she pulled her into her arms and held her close.

"Don't ever do that again! I don't want you going downtown by yourself, and I don't ever want you to not tell Jenna or me where you are."

Beth hugged her tightly. "I'm sorry, Mom. I promise I won't do anything like this again."

"Good." Cara's gaze connected with Finn's. "Thank you for bringing her home."

"No problem. I was coming here anyway."

She nodded and pulled Beth out of her embrace so she could look into her face. "What made you decide to go downtown to Finn's gym?"

"Actually, I went to see Dad."

She told them how she walked to Finn's gym after

her dad left his office. Cara's blood boiled when she thought of how Peter had left her to fend for herself. Go call a cab! The least he could have done was to make sure she got into the cab, or better yet, he could have called her.

"Why didn't you call me from Dad's office? Why did you go to Finn? The gym has to be at least fifteen blocks from the office." When she thought of the terrible things that could have happened to her daughter, she felt sick.

"I knew Finn was coming here anyway, so I thought I'd catch a ride. Isn't that right, Finn?"

He cleared his throat. "Yeah, that's right."

Cara looked at Finn, then Beth, then back to him. There was more to this story, but she wasn't sure she wanted to know. She'd already had one major emotional upset today.

"Dad said he'd stop by in a couple of days on his way home from the lake," Beth said. "And he said he's looking forward to spending two weeks with us in July." She looked up at Jenna. "Do you think he'll really come to see us when he gets back from the lake?"

Jenna shrugged. "I wouldn't count on it, squirt. Dad really doesn't care if he sees us or not. I wonder sometimes if he wishes we were never born."

"Oh, honey." Heart breaking, Cara put her arms around her oldest daughter. "Whatever your father's faults, I know he doesn't feel that way. He loves you and Beth."

Jenna pushed away from her, tears streaming down her face. "You always defend him. I don't believe he loves us, and I don't believe anything you say anymore!"

"Okay, that's enough." Finn took Jenna's hand, then reached for Beth's. "I don't know your dad, so I can't say what's going on with him. But I do know he's the one who losing out by not spending time with you two. You're amazing young women, and any man would be proud to call you his daughters. You've got an awesome mom, you've got each other, and for what it's worth, you've got me, too."

Jenna dissolved in tears as she wrapped her arms around his waist and buried her face in his chest. Beth leaned trustingly against his shoulder while he put his arms around both girls. Cara stuffed back her own tears. If she'd needed further evidence pointing to how special Finn was, she'd just had it handed to her.

Any fears she'd had about making love with him slipped away. She didn't need to be in love to have sex. She only needed to like the guy. And she liked Finn very much. He'd be the safest guy to test the waters with after her long hiatus.

Chapter Ten

Finn jogged silently beside Cara, letting his glance slide over her. She'd barely spoken since they left the condo. "Are you okay? That was a pretty intense scene earlier."

Her smile was wry. "In a way, maybe it was the best thing that could have happened. They both have more realistic views of their father now. Beth knows he's never coming back to live with us, and Jenna can stop pretending that her father's indifference doesn't hurt."

"They'll be all right. They're tough kids. And they've got you."

"And you." She smiled again, and this time it was genuine, the kind that made his heart melt and his temperature rise. "Thank you for what you said about being there for them. I know it meant a lot to them."

Finn meant every word. He'd walk through fire for Cara's daughters, just as he would for her. But how much longer would he be in their lives? Her high school reunion was only five days away. Though she'd lost only about half of the twenty-five pounds she'd originally wanted to lose, she looked amazing. Her body appeared toned and fit and excruciatingly beautiful. Even her skin looked brighter, and he knew her energy levels had increased significantly since he'd first met her.

So what did she need him for anymore?

"I've been thinking." Cara took a deep breath. "My reunion is in a few days, and I know we said we would only work together until then. But I haven't lost as much weight as I'd like to, and I'm afraid without your motivation I'll slide back into my old lazy ways. Maybe we could work out together occasionally, or I could even come to the gym sometimes. Maybe we could still be friends."

"You want to keep working together?"

She nodded, her gaze focused on her feet. "Yes."

"You want me to be your friend?"

This time she glanced briefly toward him. "Yes."

He couldn't keep his feelings bottled up any longer. "I can't be just a friend anymore, Cara."

He barely heard her whispered reply. "Oh."

He came to an abrupt halt. She stopped a few paces ahead and turned to look at him, a question in her eyes.

"I can't be just your friend because I want to be so much more." He closed the distance between them and took her hand. "I want to be your lover. Do you think that's possible?" He cupped her face with his hand, daring to hope she felt some of the deep passion he felt for her.

Her smile dazzled him. "I think that's very possible."

If he told her his true feelings, she'd bolt like a skittish rabbit. He wanted to be the man she ran to when she was scared or happy, the man she slept with every night, the person she grew old with. For now, it was enough to know she wanted to make love with him. Maybe, in time, her feelings would turn to love. And, perhaps she'd be so awed by his skillful love-making techniques that she'd fall madly in love with him.

And maybe pigs would fly.

Body thrumming with need and dousing the negative voices in his head, he pulled her close. His mouth descended on hers and he felt hunger and need in her answering kiss. The banked fires of his desire burst into a raging inferno. With a moan he pulled her against his arousal as he ravished the sweetness of her mouth.

"Finn?" she whispered as he trailed kisses down her neck.

He kissed her eyes and the bridge of her nose, his hands kneading her buttocks. "Yeah, baby?"

"We're in a public park." Laughter bubbled in her voice. "Right beside the playground."

For the first time he became aware of his surroundings. She was right; they were on a path just a few yards from a playground where children climbed on a jungle gym and parents pushed little ones on swings. A few of those parents were watching them with interest. He reluctantly released his hold on her.

"Okay, I'll concede that perhaps this is the wrong place." He took her hand and kissed each fingertip. "We need to find the right place soon to continue this...exploration."

When she trembled, Finn felt her need right down to his marrow. "Yes, we need to find the right place. Soon."

Grinning in satisfaction, he gave her one last kiss. "Let's go home. I'm starved."

She smiled and resumed her jog. Finn's feet barely touched the ground. But worry nagged him all the way back to Cara's condo. When they did find their private moment together, would she be falling at his feet, or showing him to the door?

****

The girls were setting the food on the table when they arrived back at the condo. Cara sniffed the air in appreciation. "This smells wonderful. What is it?"

"Finn's recipe for chicken cacciatore, minus the usual pasta." Jenna said. "And with it, we're having raw vegetables with low-fat yogurt dip."

"Fabulous! Believe it or not," she said with a grin, "I'm actually developing a liking for raw carrots."

She slid a glance toward Finn. The heat in his answering smile scorched her skin. One look, one smile from him made her body burn. It was scary to want a man so much.

It was even scarier to need a man so much.

As they ate, the girls regaled them with stories about their day.

"Toby Martin broke his nose playing field hockey," Beth said. "There was blood everywhere! It was way cool."

Cara grimaced. Trust a thirteen-year-old to think injuries were cool. "How'd your day go, Jenna?"

"Pretty good. I got a B-plus on my calculus exam, which is better than I thought I'd get. Oh, and Nancy is going to pick us up tomorrow and take us to Beth and Chrissy's soccer game. After the game we're going to their house to spend the night."

She set her fork back on her plate. "Whoa. When did this happen?"

"While you were out jogging," Jenna said nonchalantly. "Beth phoned Chrissy and then we talked to Nancy and decided to spend the night. She said she could bring us home in the morning before she goes to work."

"Oh. Okay."

Finn kept his gaze focused on his plate, but she saw him grin as he cut his chicken into bite-sized pieces. A delicious ripple of anticipation skittered down her back. It looked like they'd be getting their private moment sooner then expected.

As soon as they finished their dessert of fruit salad and yogurt, Finn rose from the table. "I hate to eat and run, but I've got an appointment with a client." He turned to the girls. "I guess I won't see you guys for a couple of days. Have fun on your sleepover."

"We will," Jenna said. "See you in a couple of days."

"'Bye, Finn," Beth echoed.

Cara walked him to the door, aware of her daughters' attention on them. "I'll see you tomorrow night then."

"Sure. Why don't we make it a real date?"

Her mind went blank. She hadn't expected to be wined and dined. "A date?"

"I'm sure you've heard of the concept. We get dressed up and go somewhere nice to eat. Low-cal, of course. Maybe go dancing. You said you used to like dancing. What do you think?"

"She thinks it's a great idea!"

"Jenna, I can answer for myself, thank you," Cara called over her shoulder.

"So what's your answer?"

She stared into Finn's beautiful blue eyes, and sank into their azure depths. "I think dinner and dancing sounds wonderful."

He moved in to kiss her. Cara let his lips brush

over hers in a brief touch of lips before pulling away. After accepting an official "date" with him, the kiss felt like an announcement of their couple status. Telling the world, even if it was only her daughters, that she and Finn were together felt so frightening.

Thank goodness their couple status only extended to sharing a bed.

She kissed Finn's cheek, letting her lips linger on the scratchy stubble. Breathing in the spicy scent of his aftershave, she sighed. "I'll see you tomorrow."

He cupped her face with his hands. "Tomorrow."

He kissed the end of her nose and left. She turned to see the girls watching her, grins on their faces. "If you two have all this free time to be standing around gawking, the toilets could use a good scrubbing."

"I've got calculus problems to do," Jenna said. "Gotta keep up my marks."

"And I need to pack for tomorrow night," Beth chimed in.

They quickly disappeared into their room, leaving Cara to shake her head.

She picked up the phone and punched in Nancy's number. Her friend answered on the second ring. "Hi there. So you heard the girls are spending the night here tomorrow?"

"Yeah. They just told me. Whose idea was it?"

"Totally theirs. Beth asked if I could pick them up for their soccer game. I was surprised, too, when the girls asked if they could stay overnight, but now that I think of it, it's an inspired idea."

"What do you mean?"

"They're not stupid, Cara. They know you and Finn have no privacy with them around all the time.

They're giving you two some precious time alone."

They were giving their seal of approval to her relationship with Finn. For Beth especially, that was huge. Cara wished she wasn't so damned nervous.

"It's been a long time for me. What if..." She tried to put her fears into words. "What if I've forgotten how to have sex?"

Nancy burst into laughter. "Don't worry, honey. I hear it's like riding a bike. It comes back real quick."

"I'm serious." She looked over her shoulder to make sure her daughters weren't lurking behind her. "Finn deserves someone who can give herself freely and enthusiastically. What if I don't please him?"

"What if you do? Forget about what if and just go with what feels right. Don't you find Finn attractive?"

Just thinking about his body made her weak in the knees. "Of course."

"Then don't worry about it. Be like the Nike ad and just do it."

"Just do it, huh?"

"Best advice I've ever given you. When was the last time you had mind-blowing sex?"

"Way too long ago. Thanks for looking after the girls. And thanks for the pep talk."

"No problem. Have fun."

Cara carefully replaced the receiver. *Go with what feels right?* When she thought of it that way she knew Finn was everything she wanted. He was funny and kind and sexy as hell. His kisses made her go up in flames, and just thinking of his touches made her go damp.

Finn was exactly right.

She hurried to her room, hoping she could find

some sexy underwear tucked beneath the vast collection of granny panties in her drawer.

****

Finn watched candlelight turn Cara's hazel eyes to warm, rich amber. Her fair skin glowed with good health and her glorious blonde hair hung in thick waves around her shoulders. Seeing it unbound from its usual ponytail aroused him more than he could have imagined.

And he'd never been more nervous in his entire life. "Would you like another glass of wine?"

"No thanks. My trainer's a real stickler about calorie intake," she said. "He'd probably make me run an extra mile or two tomorrow if I had a second glass."

"Sounds like a real killjoy."

"Actually, he's terrific." She reached across the table to take his hand. "He's helped me get into shape when I thought I couldn't do it. He makes me feel like I can do anything I set my mind to."

Finn traced the contour of her fingers, marveling at the beauty of her hands and the silkiness of her skin. Everything about her was exquisite. "Tell me more."

Her low, throaty chuckle went straight to his groin. "He's very funny and makes me laugh all the time. He's probably the kindest man I've ever known. I can't express how grateful I am for the thoughtfulness he's shown my daughters."

"Anything else you want to add?"

"Hmm... Let me think. No, that's about it. Great guy, funny, kind. Oh, yeah, I forgot. Sexy as hell."

"You think I'm sexy?"

"Of course I do. Everybody does. Don't you know how gorgeous and sexy you are?"

Despite the weight loss, despite the rigorous training and exercise, sometimes he still felt like the fat kid who never got picked for sports, the one everybody made fun of.

Finn looked toward the dance floor where a few couples swayed to the music of the jazz quartet playing a slow, sad tune. He squeezed her hand. "Would you like to dance?"

"I'd love to."

He led her out on the floor and she stepped into his arms. It was heaven to hold her. The intoxicating scent of jasmine filled his senses. Finn let his hand rest on the small of her back.

"You look incredible tonight."

The black sleeveless dress hugged Cara in all the right places, allowing a tantalizing but demure show of cleavage and a breathtaking view of her bare back. She looked up into his eyes and smiled. "Thanks. I've had this dress for a while, but I haven't been able to fit into it again until now. One more thing I'm thankful to you for."

"I'm pretty thankful myself right now."

Cara stepped closer, molding herself to him. "Thank you, Finn."

He held her tighter, breathing in her enthralling scent. He wanted so much more from her than gratitude.

He wanted her love.

She'd come to him at one of the lowest points in her life, when she felt most vulnerable. Now that her confidence had returned, would she need him anymore?

He didn't want to think about that. For tonight, all he wanted to think about was the beautiful woman in his arms.

"Finn?"

"Yes?"

"This evening was wonderful. Everything—the food, the wine, the music—was beautiful. It's been a very long time since I've been out on a date."

He brushed his lips against hers. Her soft mouth opened slightly and her tongue touched his lips. Flames exploded inside him. He opened his mouth to hers, exploring her sweetness, loving the taste of wine that lingered on her lips. At last he pulled away, breathless, and rested his forehead against hers.

"We've got to stop making a spectacle of ourselves in public."

"Yes." He heard her deep intake of breath. "So why don't we go somewhere private? Like your place."

He leaned back so he could look in her eyes. "You mean that?"

"Of course I do. I don't take this stuff lightly. I want to make love with you."

Caught between elation and absolute terror, he pushed fear aside and took her hand. "Let's go."

He settled their bill and, with Cara's hand still in his, headed to the parking lot. He drove as quickly as he safely could, and in a short time they arrived at his house. "Here we are."

Finn loved his place but wondered what Cara saw when she looked at the modest two-story home. He stepped out of his car and opened the passenger door, giving her his hand to help her out.

"So this is your place," she said.

"Be it ever so humble."

"I think it's adorable." She wound her arms around

his neck. "Just like you."

He bent to kiss her, and the inferno he'd felt in the restaurant burst back into life.

"Let's get inside. Quick."

"Good idea."

He unlocked the door with trembling hands and let Cara in. She looked around his living room with appreciation. "This is really nice. Very minimalist, very uncluttered. I like it."

He pulled her against his rapidly growing arousal. If they waited too long, he might explode. Again. "Do you really want to discuss the decor?"

She laughed. "Not unless we're discussing the color scheme in your bedroom. Where is it?"

"Upstairs." She shrieked as he swept her into his arms. "Come with me."

Laughing, she said, "Do I have a choice?"

Cara felt as light as a feather as he carried her up the stairs. In his advanced state of arousal, he probably could have carried her up the stairs of the Empire State Building without breaking a sweat.

He set her carefully on the bed, and as he began stripping off his shirt and tie, one of the buttons flew off.

"My goodness, you're in a hurry. What's your rush? We've got all night."

He closed his eyes and fought for control. He'd never last that long.

"Finn? What's wrong?"

"Nothing. I'm fine."

"No, you're not." She got to her feet and stood beside him, concern etched on her face. "I think I know you well enough to tell when you're upset. Spill it."

He considered making another denial, but thought better of it when he looked into her face. She deserved to know the truth. He fought his embarrassment and the demands of his body. He was hanging on by a thread. "I haven't exactly been honest with you."

"You're not involved with someone else, are you?" She looked around the room as if searching for evidence of a female occupant.

"No, of course not. Nothing like that." He pushed his hand through his hair. "God, this is embarrassing."

"Finn, you're scaring me. What's wrong?"

He took her hand and made her sit on the edge of the bed next to him. He swallowed and took a deep breath.

"Cara, I'm a...a..."

"A what? Please, just spit it out!"

"I'm a virgin."

Chapter Eleven

"What did you say?"

This time he shouted it. "I'm a virgin!"

His admission was greeted with stunned silence. Cara's eyes were wide, her eyebrows raised into her hairline.

"Surprise!"

She shook her head. "No kidding. That's the last thing I expected. Why didn't you tell me this before?"

"It's too humiliating."

He couldn't look at her. He felt her hand on his shoulder. "Tell me what happened."

"Nothing happened. That's the problem."

"Finn."

He risked a glance at her, and her expression told him she wouldn't tolerate evasion. But he also saw kindness in her eyes, and concern. He took a deep breath before beginning.

"Like I told you, I decided to lose weight and get healthy on my thirtieth birthday, five years ago. Up until that time I wasn't what you'd call a chick magnet. You saw the pictures."

"Maybe you didn't have a girlfriend then, but surely after you lost the weight, lots of women must have been interested in you."

"They were interested. It took over two years to lose the weight and get into shape. Much to my surprise, women started noticing me. I'd have gorgeous females coming up to me at the gym and giving me their phone numbers. And believe me, they made it very clear they wanted nothing more than a little tumble and that was exactly what I wanted, too. So I made a date with one woman. We were on her bed kissing, and she touched me and I sort of...went off."

"Premature ejaculation?"

He nodded. The embarrassment of that moment still stung. "That was humiliating enough, but then she laughed. I grabbed my clothes and got the hell out of there."

"And so you've been too embarrassed to be with another woman since."

"Not quite," Finn admitted. "There was someone else. From my Weight Watchers group. She seemed nice, so I thought maybe things would work out this time. But the same thing happened. This time instead of laughing the woman was totally disgusted. She actually threw me out. I was so embarrassed I quit the group so I never had to face her again."

"Oh, Finn, I'm sorry. That must have been awful for you."

He got to his feet. "I'm sorry I brought you here under false circumstances. I'll take you home now."

"Did I say I wanted to go home?"

"Well, no, but—"

She stood and wound her arms around his neck, her body touching his from chest to thigh. "Nothing changed. I still want to make love with you."

"Even if, you know, I get to the finish line a little ahead of schedule?"

She laughed her sexy, throaty laugh once more. His

arousal pushed painfully against the zipper of his pants. "If that happens, then I guess all we can do is start over again."

He looked away. "I couldn't bear to humiliate myself with you."

She placed her hands on either side of his face and forced him to look at her. "No matter what happens, I don't ever want you to feel that way with me. Don't you know what a gift you're giving me? You're asking me to be your first. I'm truly humbled by such an honor."

He didn't know what to say. All he knew was that he loved Cara even more than he did before. He desperately wanted to tell her how he felt, but didn't want to ruin the moment. The last thing he wanted was to make her feel awkward.

He was awkward enough for both of them.

"You're amazing."

Sliding her hands under his open shirt, she pushed it from his shoulders. She kissed his chest, licking his nipples and gently nipping them with her teeth. Finn clutched her shoulders.

"I don't know if I can hold on much longer."

"Don't worry. Like I said, we've got all night."

She reached behind her back to unzip her dress. Finn snapped on the lamp next to his bed. She looked up at him in surprise, her arms crossed over her breasts.

"What are you doing? Why did you turn the lamp on?"

He touched her hair, wrapping a silky strand around his finger. "I want to see you. You're beautiful, Cara."

"Turn it off, please!"

He was surprised by her vehemence. He turned off the lamp, plunging the room into darkness once more. The only illumination came through the window from the street light in front of his house. But it was enough for him to see Cara's lush curves as she let the dress fall to the floor. When she unhooked her bra, letting her full breasts spill forward, he groaned with need. She reached for him.

"Let me undress you."

She stepped close, letting her breasts brush his bare chest as she unbuckled his belt. Finn shuddered. He closed his eyes and concentrated on hanging on. Cara unzipped his pants and pushed them down his hips, her hands squeezing his buttocks and skimming his belly, his thighs.

"I can't wait either. Do you have some protection?"

"Yes."

He reached into the nightstand and pulled out a condom from the box he'd bought that afternoon in hopes the evening would end like this. His hands shook as he tried to open the package. Cara took it from him.

"Let me do it."

Wordlessly he handed her the package, heart pounding and erratic breathing totally out of control. When he pushed his briefs past his hips, his penis sprang free, hard and throbbing.

Cara slipped off her panties, letting them fall to the floor to pool at her feet. In the semi-darkness he made out the outline of her generous curves and the tantalizing glimpse of the triangle of hair at the apex of her thighs. He wished she'd let him see her in the light, but he'd take whatever she was willing to give. She extended her hand to him, and Finn grasped it, holding tight as she led him to his bed. She pulled back the covers and gently pushed him onto the sheets, then straddled his hips. Opening the Mylar package containing the condom, she pulled it out and began to put it on him. But the instant she touched him, he exploded. He groaned in agony, humiliation making him close his eyes and turn away from her. He couldn't bear to see the pity on her face.

He felt her leave the bed and his throat closed. What could he say to her? Would this always happen to him? If it did, maybe he should seriously think about taking a vow of celibacy. It had to be better than humiliating himself like this over and over. Did monks still wear long black robes?

A moment later, she returned to the bed. He opened his eyes when he felt a warm, damp cloth touching his lower belly. "What are you doing?"

He could see Cara's smile in the dim light. "Just cleaning you up a bit."

"I thought you'd left." He flung an arm across his eyes. "I wouldn't blame you if you had."

"Why would I leave?"

Finn took a sharp intake of breath as her finger traced the inside of his thigh, trailing upward toward his penis. He removed his arm and opened his eyes, leaning on his elbows to look at her.

"I told you that if you came a little before schedule, we'd just have to start all over again," she said. "That's what I intend to do."

Finn grabbed her hand, stopping her from touching him again. "I don't want pity."

She laughed the low throaty chuckle that never failed to turn him on. "What I feel right now has very little to do with pity. I want to touch you everywhere, kiss you everywhere. I want to feel you inside me." He felt the tremble that coursed through her body. "I can't tell you how much I want that. Please, Finn, let me love you."

He released her hand. "What do you want me to do?"

"For now, just relax."

He leaned back against the pillows and watched her. She stretched out next to him, propping her head with one hand, and using the other to touch him.

"You're so incredibly beautiful," she said, running a finger around his right nipple. "And your skin is so soft. I didn't expect that."

She kissed the hardened nipples, licking and suckling until he moaned. Straddling his hips once more, she kissed her way down his body. When she reached his flaccid penis she looked up at him and smiled. "May I taste more of you?"

Before he could answer, she lowered her head and ran her tongue down the length of his penis. Finn groaned and gripped the sheets, feeling himself stir to life. Would he hold on this time?

She looked up at him again. "You're incredible, Finn. I want all of you. Please let me have all of you."

He nodded, his body shaking with desire. She lowered her head once more, taking him into her mouth. Her tongue swirled around the end of his penis, teasing and tempting. His mind went blank, his only thought Cara's exquisite seduction and his body's enthusiastic reaction.

A moment later she lifted her head. "You're ready for me, Finn, and I am so ready for you."

She reached for the condom she'd placed on the night table, and slowly sheathed him. Finn groaned at the beautiful torture of her touch. And then she impaled herself on him. He held his breath, afraid he would reach his climax prematurely and spoil her enjoyment.

At least he hoped she was enjoying herself. From the way she threw back her head as she rode him, moaning her pleasure and calling his name, he guessed he was doing all right. His own pleasure was immeasurable. He never imagined anything could feel as magnificent as making love to Cara. He was inside her so deep he could swear he felt her heart beating, so deep he didn't know where he ended and she began. He loved her more now than he'd ever thought possible.

She began to quiver. A moment later she screamed her release. With one final thrust, Finn reached his own climax. Wave after wave crashed over him as an endless sea of passion tossed him mercilessly about. When it finally ended, she folded herself over him and he held her, utterly exhausted but completely sated.

Nothing in his life compared to making love with her.

****

Cara woke to the delicious sensation of being cocooned in Finn's warm arms. The room was dark; the clock beside his bed read three a.m. She sighed and snuggled closer, breathing in his clean, masculine scent.

She could scarcely believe how she'd seduced Finn the previous evening. She'd never been so bold before, and just thinking about it made her face heat in a blush. But she'd never felt so desired before. He made her feel powerful, sexy, unstoppable. With Finn, she could almost believe she was beautiful.

He stirred, and in the faint light, she saw his eyes flutter open and focus on her face. "Hi."

"Hi. What time is it?"

"About three a.m. Go back to sleep."

She ran her fingertips over his face, loving the feeling of the stubble on his skin. Tenderness swamped her. Making love with Finn was supposed to be a bit of fun. She wasn't supposed to feel such overwhelming joy at being in his arms.

She wasn't supposed to be thinking about forever.

"Hmmm, that feels good," he said, opening his eyes once more. He kissed the end of her nose, and his hands began an exploration of her body. "What do you like, Cara?"

Her breath caught as he touched the underside of her breast with his thumb. "What do you mean?"

"How do you like to be touched? Where do you like to be kissed?"

Everywhere, if it's by you. "I don't know."

"Trust me, Cara. You can tell me anything."

He kissed the corner of her mouth and she sighed. "I like it when you touch my breasts."

He gently kneaded her right breast, rolling the nipple between his thumb and forefinger. "Like this?" He rolled her on her back, gently kissing each breast in turn. She writhed beneath him, wanting more.

"Tell me what you want, sweetheart," he whispered. He licked the nipple, swirling his tongue around the hardened peak, and sending a jolt of electricity straight to her womb. "Do you want more?"

"Yes, yes!"

He took first one breast and then the other into his mouth, suckling, pulling, laving, gently biting. Moisture pooled between her thighs. Urgency built inside her until she could stand no more.

"Please, touch me."

"Show me what to do, where to touch you."

She guided his hand until his clever fingers found her most sensitive spot. Her breath caught as he instinctively massaged the nub, building the pleasure until she convulsed around his fingers. She cried out her release. "Finn! Oh, God, Finn!"

He muffled her cries with a deep kiss, his tongue mating with hers, dancing and fighting. The pressure she'd thought sated roared back to life, her body demanding more. "Please, Finn."

"Tell me what you want, baby."

"Finn—"

"You can tell me anything, Cara. There's nothing we can't say to each other, nothing we won't do for each other. Do you trust me?"

In that moment she would have followed him anywhere, done anything for him. "Yes."

"Then tell me, sweetheart. What do you want me to do?"

"I want you to…put your mouth where your finger has just been."

She searched his face in the pale light for a look of disgust, but instead he grinned. "Remember, I'm new at this."

"You seem to be catching on fast."

He chuckled, then kissed his way down her body until he reached the apex of her thighs. Gently, he spread her legs and touched his tongue to her most sensitive spot. She moaned, arching her back in an effort to bring him closer. The sensation was exquisite.

The tension built and built until once more her release came, more powerful than ever before.

This is what it's supposed to feel like.

He briefly left the bed, reaching into his drawer for another condom. He quickly sheathed himself and came back to the bed, straddling her once more.

"Cara."

He brushed her hair from her face with infinite tenderness. She wrapped her legs around him as he slipped inside her. It felt so good, so *right.*

He pushed into her, slowly at first, but then gradually building to a frenzy that enveloped them until they both found their release, together.

****

The morning sun streaming through the window woke Cara from a dead sleep. For several seconds she stared at the unfamiliar ceiling, unable to get her bearings. Where the hell was she? Then she remembered she was in Finn's house, in his bed. The incredible events of the previous night flooded back, overwhelming her once more. After the initial awkwardness, the sex had been amazing, but even more amazing was the intimacy, the closeness she'd shared with Finn.

It had been the first time she'd been asked what she liked, where she wanted to be touched, what her partner could do to give her more pleasure. For the first time, she'd felt free to ask for what she really wanted. The experience had been incredibly liberating.

Not to mention incredibly sexy.

Thinking about the previous night made her want Finn again. She rolled over, hoping to wake him to make love once more. But Finn's side of the bed was empty, the sheets cold. Panic gripped her. Had he left? Would he leave without saying goodbye? Were they over before they'd even begun?

She sat up, wrapping the sheet around her breasts. She was being ridiculous. There was probably a perfectly rational reason why he was out of bed by— she glanced at the clock next to the bed—6:30 a.m. and hadn't woken her to let her know.

A not-so-rational voice in her head screamed that she was being abandoned all over again.

No, Finn wouldn't leave her, not like this, without a word of explanation.

Willing her heart to slow to a normal beat, she reclined against the pillow once more. He wasn't like Peter. He was kind and honorable. So what if he wasn't there when she woke up? He didn't have to account to her for his every move.

She relaxed against the pillows and smiled to herself. She really was a dork. An insecure, silly dork.

The door opened and Finn quietly stepped inside carrying a tray with two cups of coffee. Cara nearly wept in relief when she saw him.

"Hey, you're awake. You looked so peaceful I didn't have the heart to wake you."

She pulled the sheet a little more securely around her breasts. "You probably should have. I should be there when Nancy brings the girls home."

"I doubt they're even awake." He set the tray on the night table and passed her a mug. "Would you like coffee? One milk no sugar, the way you like it."

He remembered. Her heart did a little flip-flop. She took the mug from him. "Thanks."

Coming to sit beside her on the bed, he tugged

gently at the corner of her sheet. "It's kind of late to cover up now, don't you think? I've kind of seen everything already."

She slapped at his hand. "Don't be crude."

"Cara, I'm joking. What's the matter?"

"Nothing. Why are you up so early?"

"I have to meet a client at the gym before she goes to work."

He was leaving her to meet with another woman. She knew it wasn't like that, but still she let the thought fuel her anger. "Fine."

"What's the matter?"

She had no idea. All she knew was that she'd needed him to be with her when she woke this morning and when he wasn't, all her old fears rose to the surface. "Nothing."

"Are you sorry about last night?"

Her head rose sharply. He looked away, not meeting her gaze. However mixed up she felt this morning, she couldn't let Finn feel that he'd somehow failed her. Setting her mug on the night table on her side of the bed, she caressed his unshaven cheek.

"Of course I'm not sorry. I loved our night together. Don't mind me, Finn. I'm in a mood this morning."

He tugged at her sheet once more. "Then let go of the sheet and let me hold you before I have to go."

Cara held her sheet tighter. It was one thing to get undressed in the dark and another to let him see her body in the cruel light of day. "No, please. I'd rather not."

Would he look at her in the cold morning light and see all the imperfections and scars that came with forty-three years of living? Would he look at her and want to trade her in for a newer model?

"I think you're beautiful. You know that, don't you?"

No, she really didn't know that, but she nodded anyway. What happened when he woke up one morning and realized that she had a few more lines on her face? Would he still think she was beautiful or would he tire of her, just as Peter had?

Finn put his arm around her. "Do you wake up in a mood like this every morning?"

She smiled against his shoulder and resolved to enjoy whatever time they had together. It was only a bit of fun, after all. "Only when I've made love to an incredibly handsome man the previous evening."

He chuckled, his breath tickling her ear. "Whatever it is, it's going to be okay. We'll work it out. Together." He kissed her hair. "I've been thinking. Why don't I go to your reunion with you?"

She stiffened. "Why would you want to do that? You won't know anyone there."

"I just want to support you, make sure you're all right. And maybe I want to show the world that we're together now. That we're a couple."

Cara sat up straight and stared at him. It wasn't supposed to be like this. She'd wanted simple, uncomplicated, safe. But how could she stay safe, how could she protect her heart, when he looked at her with such tenderness? She stuffed down her panic as she wrapped the sheet firmly around herself and slid from the bed.

"We're getting awfully serious all of a sudden. I mean, we've only had one night together." She picked up her underwear from the floor where she'd dropped it the night before. The memory almost made her burst into tears.

"It was a pretty wonderful night. I'm hoping for many repeat performances." His face sobered as he closed the distance between them. "I want to be with you, be part of your life."

She evaded him, and began to pace the small bedroom. "Don't get me wrong. Last night was great, but I'm not looking for long-term commitment, just some fun sex."

"I want fun sex, too, but I want it only with you. And I want more than just sex, Cara. I want you. I love you."

Oh no, he'd gone and done it. He'd said the L-word. Her hands shook as she gripped her sheet. "I don't know if I can give you more. If that's what you want, perhaps we should end it right now, before somebody gets hurt."

Surprise and hurt flashed across Finn's face and tore at her heart. She wanted to take it all back, but it was too late. Besides, now that he'd learned a little about pleasing a woman, he'd be anxious to try out his new-found skills on younger, more beautiful women. She wouldn't keep him interested long, and he'd be anxious to move on. She was doing him a favor.

Do you really believe that, Cara?

"Is that what you want? You want to end it now?"

No! No! No!

She nodded. "Maybe that would be best."

"If that's what you really want, I'll go. Say goodbye to the girls for me." He turned to leave. As he opened the door, he faced her once more. "It's not true,

124

you know. What we have together is more than just fun sex, and I think you know that. I love you, probably have since I first met you at the TV station. But if a life with me truly isn't what you want, I can't force you to feel differently. Be happy, Cara."

He left the bedroom and quietly closed the door behind him. Cara's legs buckled beneath her. Dear God, had she done the right thing?

She'd done the only thing she could to keep her heart safe. If she let herself fall in love with him, it would hurt so much more when he left.

Chapter Twelve

Three days and Finn didn't call.

Cara shook her head. Of course he hadn't called. She'd told him to go away. He was only doing what she'd asked.

So why did she feel so awful?

She pulled the dress she'd bought for her fortieth birthday from her closet, preparing to get ready for the high school reunion dinner at the Summerville Inn. She hugged the dress close to her, remembering the last time she'd worn it, three nights ago on her date with Finn. She remembered the feel of his hand on her bare back, the gleam of the candlelight in his eyes, the way he'd undressed her as if he was opening a precious gift.

Cara buried her face in the black silk. She wouldn't cry, not anymore, or else she wouldn't be able to make it through the reunion.

The phone rang, and she groaned when she saw her mother's telephone number pop up on the screen. Her mother was the last person she wanted to speak to today. But if she didn't answer now there'd be more questions: *where were you, who were you with, what did you do?*

With a sigh, she picked up the receiver. "Hello, Mom."

"Cara, I have to tell you I'm mortified, simply mortified!"

"I believe the customary telephone greeting is 'Hello,' Mother."

Mariette ignored her. "My friend Latisha Price and her husband were dining at the Plaza Restaurant the other night, when who should they see on the dance floor grinding against some young buck but my daughter! She said it was a shameful public display."

For a full ten seconds Cara didn't speak, or move, or breathe. Inside her heart, a door slammed shut. She hit a wall, reached the end of her rope, arrived at the end of the line.

"Well?" Mariette demanded. "What do you have to say for yourself?"

"I don't have anything to say. It's not anybody's damn business who I dance with or who I kiss, Mother."

"When your actions reflect on me and your father, it certainly is my business! And I'll thank you to keep a civil tongue in your head. Swearing is crass."

"Then I guess I'm pretty god-damn crass, because I like to swear, and I like to have sex with men. That's right, Mother. Your daughter is a huge slut! I slow-danced with an extremely handsome younger man and then I went home with him and had the best, most astonishing sex I've ever had in my life. I bloody banged his brains out, and if I had the chance, I'd do it all over again."

She heard Mariette's shocked intake of breath. "My God, Cara! What will people think?"

"Frankly, Mother, I don't give a god-damn what you or Latisha Price or anyone else thinks of me. I've had it with trying to live up to your impossible standards and your never-ending demands. You're squeezing the life out of me, and I can't take it anymore!"

"I'll call you back when you've come to your senses and are ready to apologize."

"No, you won't. First of all, I finally *have* come to my senses, and secondly, I'm never going to apologize. For too many years you've made me feel bad for just being me, and I don't have to live like that anymore. Goodbye, Mother."

She hung up the phone and unplugged the jack from the wall in case her mother tried to call back. On Monday she'd get a new, unlisted number. For a moment, Cara stood hugging herself in the middle of her bedroom, the enormity of what she'd done sinking in. Then the tears came, tears of sweet relief. She felt as if a staggering weight had been lifted from her shoulders and that she was free for the first time in her life. Finn had been right. She was stronger than she thought.

Beth knocked on her door and entered before Cara could tell her to wait. She flopped onto the bed and stared at the ceiling. "I just talked to Finn on the phone and asked him to come over, but he said he couldn't. Why doesn't he want to see us anymore?"

Cara wiped away the last of her tears. *What a day.* "Beth, I told you, now that this reunion is almost here, Finn and I won't be working together anymore. Please don't phone him again."

"I don't understand. I thought he was our friend."

"He was, sweetheart, but now it's over."

"No, it's not fair! Why does everybody leave us?"

She flung one arm over her eyes and began to cry. Cara tossed her dress onto a chair and went to her daughter, her heart breaking. She held her close. "Beth, honey, please don't cry. Everything will be okay."

"No, it won't! You said that when Dad left, but everything hasn't been okay. He never calls and we hardly see him. And now the same thing is going to happen with Finn. I hate him! I wish we'd never met him!"

Cara was shocked at her anger. "Sweetheart, you can't mean that."

"Yes, I do! I'm never going to love anybody but you and Jenna. You're the only ones who've never left me. I'm never going to have a boyfriend or get married, because husbands and boyfriends always leave and make you unhappy. It's better to be alone."

Dear God, is this what she'd taught her daughters? That a life alone was preferable to taking a chance on love? That the joy of having a family and children wasn't worth the risk?

"Beth, you're so wrong. Your dad and I had a lot of good years and good times. And best of all, we had you two girls. But sometimes people grow apart and want different things, and they don't stay together forever and ever. That doesn't mean that their marriage was wrong in the first place. No one can know what's going to happen in the future."

"What about Finn? He said he loved you and that he never wanted to hurt you. He told me he wanted to marry you. But then he just left. I thought he'd be with us forever."

She hugged Beth a little closer. "Finn told you he loved me?"

"Yeah. That day I went to his gym."

"Oh, sweetheart, don't blame Finn. It's not his

fault."

"But why did he leave?"

She couldn't let Beth think Finn was to blame. But she couldn't bring herself to tell the whole story either. "It didn't work out between us. I'm sorry you were hurt."

"I liked him."

Cara stroked her hair. "I know, baby." *So did I.*

Jenna walked into the bedroom. "Mom, Nancy just sent me a text message. She's wondering what time you're going to drop us off before you go to the reunion." She looked at Beth curled in Cara's arms. "What's going on?"

"Beth's upset about Finn."

Jenna's lips formed a hard, angry line. "I hate men. They make a lot of promises and then they let you down."

"Jenna!"

"It's true, isn't it? First Dad and now Finn. Eventually they all leave."

"That's not true. Finn didn't leave because he wanted to. He left because I told him to go. So if you want to be angry with someone, be angry with me. But don't blame him."

"Why would you tell him to go?" Jenna asked, disbelief etched on her face.

"I had my reasons. Now, please go, so I can get dressed."

Beth hauled herself off the bed and took Jenna's hand. Silently, they left Cara's room and closed the door. She pinched her eyes closed, trying to hold back the dam of tears that threatened to break inside her heart.

Eventually she gained control of herself once more. She slid the black dress over her head and then did her best to repair her hair and makeup. She took one last look at herself in the mirror before she headed out the door. A woman with a haunted expression stared back at her.

She'd done so many things wrong in her life, but she worried that her biggest mistake might be the unintended lessons she'd taught her daughters about love.

****

Welcome Summerville High School Class of '85!

The giant banner told her she was in the right place. Tiny twinkling lights decorated the entrance to the Summerville Inn, attempting to create a fun and carefree atmosphere. Cara sighed. She felt anything but fun and carefree right now. But she entered the hotel and pasted a smile on her face as she approached the registration desk.

"Hi, I'm Cara McLeod, or I guess you might have me down as Cara Blackwell," she said, using her maiden name.

"Here you are." The woman handed her a name tag, then tilted her head to observe her, her eyes glittering with curiosity. "Weren't you on the cheerleading squad in senior year? You went out with the quarterback, didn't you? Whatever happened to him?"

"I married him. And then divorced him." Cara had a feeling this woman already knew the answer before she asked the question. She bent slightly to observe her name tag. Nadine Archer. Now it all made sense.

"Nice to see you again." She was determined to

play nice even though Nadine had been the school's biggest gossip in high school. Perhaps she'd changed.

"I saw your ex here earlier with a very young woman," she whispered conspiratorially.

Or maybe not.

Nadine had not been nicknamed "the Mouth" for nothing. Cara glanced at her overdone makeup and strapless, sparkly silver dress and almost felt sorry for her. She looked like a forty-three-year-old woman desperately trying to look twenty-three in a dress two sizes too small.

"So, what are you doing these days? Weren't you voted most likely to have the perfect marriage?" The sarcasm dripped from her words. Cara chose to ignore it.

"I work in television. I host a local events show in Rochester." Nadine didn't have to know that up until two weeks ago she'd been a lowly junior assistant.

A tiny, curly-haired woman stepped up to the registration desk. "Cara? Cara Blackwell? Oh, it is you!"

"Oh, my God!"

Molly Carter launched herself into Cara's arms. She hugged her back, glad to see a friendly face. Molly had been a friend to everyone, refusing to be pigeonholed into any one clique. Cara had admired her independent spirit back in high school.

"It's lovely to see you. I saw you the other day on *Rochester Noon.* You were terrific! We always knew you'd do something fun!"

"Thanks. I'm glad you liked the show. It can be stressful at times, but mostly it's a lot of fun. What are you doing these days? Solving the Mideast crisis?

Negotiating world peace?"

Molly laughed. "Not quite. My husband Ned and I are foster parents. We look after hard-to-place children."

"Somehow, I am not surprised. It sounds like the perfect job for you. And you married Ned McCarthy from high school?"

Before Molly could speak, Nadine butted in. "Yes, Molly and Ned have been married forever. Old news. Molly, did you hear about Cara's ex, Peter McLeod? He's here with his girlfriend." She leaned toward them, and then glanced over her shoulder as if she didn't want anyone to overhear her.

As if.

"Peter's girlfriend is awfully young, don't you think? Too young for a man in his forties. He certainly can't want anything but s-e-x from her."

From the gleam in her eye, she knew Nadine was looking for a reaction from her, something juicy and lurid that she could spread amongst the rest of the attendees. *Cara Blackwell's ex is dating a girl half his age and she is crushed. So much for the girl most likely.*

She wouldn't give the bitch the satisfaction.

"Peter's girlfriend is a lovely woman. Actually, we're thinking of forming a threesome. It's been wonderful seeing you, Nadine."

She left the Mouth with her lips flapping like a landed fish. Cara winked at Molly, whose eyes twinkled with merriment, clearly catching the joke. If Nadine was going to gossip, she might as well have something sensational to talk about.

She wandered into the huge ballroom and headed to the bar to grab a glass of white wine. She paid for her drink and then checked her watch, wondering how long until dinner was served and she could make her escape.

Someone jostled her arm, causing her to spill wine onto the floor and over her shoe.

"Oh gosh, I'm so sorry," the man said. He pulled a cloth hankie from his pocket and dabbed at her wet hand. "Can I buy you another drink, new shoes?"

Cara laughed. "No, I'm sure that won't be necessary. Last time I checked, I didn't melt when I got wet. But I will borrow that hankie for a moment."

He handed it to her. "Yes, please, be my guest."

She passed him her wine glass and then wiped her wet hand before stooping to wipe the wine from her open-toed shoe. She hoped this incident wasn't an indication of what the rest of the evening had in store for her.

She handed back the hankie. "Thanks for the loan. I'm sorry it's a bit wet."

"No problem. My wife insists I carry one at all times because I usually need it to clean up some mess I've made." He smiled shyly. "I'm a bit of klutz, you see."

"Your secret is safe with me. I promise I won't tell your wife." She looked at his name tag. *Martin Baranski.* "Martin, of course. I should have recognized you. You were our resident scientific genius. How are you?"

"I'm well. I recognized you right away, Cara. You haven't changed since high school."

"Obviously, you need new glasses, but thank you. So what are you doing these days?"

"I work at NASA in Houston."

Cara's eyes widened. "Wow, that's fantastic. I

knew you were smart, but an honest-to-goodness rocket scientist is very cool."

"How about you? You were the one voted most likely to succeed, our senior year. What big things have you accomplished? Running any Fortune 500 companies?"

"No, not quite. I work at a television station. Actually, I'm getting my life back together since my divorce. And my biggest accomplishment is raising my two daughters alone."

Martin nodded in understanding, but there was no pity in his eyes, or any sense that he was happy about her comeuppance in life. "How would you like to meet my wife? I think you know her, Mitzi Goldberg?"

"Mitzi? Of course! I'd love to see her! I didn't know you two had married."

"We ended up at the same undergraduate university in Syracuse. And the rest is history, as they say."

She followed Martin to a table across the ballroom, where a dark woman with glasses was holding court with several people she didn't recognize.

"Mitzi, look who I dumped wine on at the bar."

Mitzi turned to look at her, and Cara could almost hear the wheels in her brain churning as she tried to place her. Suddenly her face lit in recognition. "Cara? Cara Blackwell." She extended her hand to her. "Let me look at you. My God, girl, you're even more beautiful than you were in high school, if that's possible. You truly are Miss New York."

She laughed at Mitzi's old nickname for her. She bent to hug her, feeling close to tears. "It's so wonderful to see you. I wish I hadn't lost contact with you, and not just because you're good for my ego."

"Are you here alone?" She looked around Cara's shoulder, checking for anyone who might be lurking behind her. "No significant other with you?"

She immediately thought of Finn, and her smile wobbled. "I'm here alone."

How sad that sounded.

"Then come sit with us and I'll introduce you to our friends."

She pushed away from the table, and for the first time Cara noticed she was in a wheel chair. Her breath caught in her throat.

Mitzi must have seen the look on her face. "I've had some health issues recently. The chair just makes it easier to get around."

She nodded. Mitzi sounded so matter of fact, as if it were nothing to be confined to a wheel chair. But if her old friend wasn't making a big deal of it, then neither would she.

She introduced Cara around the table to a group of people she vaguely remembered from high school but hadn't really known. They'd all been science geeks and belonged to various scientific clubs, which meant she rarely crossed paths with them. And even if she had, she likely wouldn't have given them the time of day back then, she thought sadly.

A few moments later, dinner was served. Cara barely tasted the chicken. Through the speeches that followed the dinner, she kept wondering where Finn was this evening, how he was feeling. Was he with someone else tonight?

The speeches ended, and servers gathered the dishes. Tables were moved to make room for dancing. Cara turned to Mitzi and Martin, trying to shake off her melancholy mood. "It's nice that all your friends could make it to the reunion."

"The ten of us get together somewhere every year for our own little reunion, so we figured why not kill two birds with one stone this year and come to Summerville for the twenty-fifth," Mitzi said.

"You've all kept in touch since high school?"

"Some of us went to university together; Tom and I even worked together for a while. Old friends are the best friends. You don't have to explain anything to them. They just know." Mitzi shared a smile with Martin before turning back to Cara. "How about you? Have you kept in touch with any of your old friends from high school?"

"No, not at all. Well, other than my ex-husband Peter."

"The quarterback, right?"

"Right. We were married for almost twenty years." She pulled a picture of the girls from her purse. "These are our two daughters, Jenna and Beth, the best things to come out of that marriage."

Mitzi examined the picture closely, holding it for a long time. She handed it to Martin and then smiled at Cara. "They're beautiful girls. You must be very proud."

"I am. They're terrific kids. How about you two? Do you have kids?"

A shadow passed over Mitzi's face but she recovered quickly. "No, unfortunately we were never able to have children."

"I'm sorry." Cara felt a little awkward. It was obvious from Mitzi's reaction that she'd wanted children. She scrambled for a new topic. "How long have you two been married?"

"One year," Martin said proudly. "In fact tomorrow is our first anniversary."

"Just one year? Even though you've known each other all this time?"

"There's no sense rushing these things," Mitzi said with a smile. She took Cara's hand. "Actually, a year ago I was told I had terminal cancer and I only had about six months to live. I've already exceeded the doctors' expectations."

The news overwhelmed Cara. Would she have the courage and grace that Mitzi had if she were faced with such news?

"You always were a fighter," Martin said, kissing her cheek. "We'd been living together for fifteen years before that, but when Mitzi got the diagnosis, I decided it was time to make an honest woman of her."

"I'm so sorry," Cara said. Sorry seemed totally inadequate, but it was all she had.

"We've made our peace with the news," Mitzi said, patting Cara's hand. "All we want to do now is to enjoy the time we have left."

"And you came all the way from Houston to Summerville for this reunion. Wasn't the trip difficult?"

"I'll admit it was tiring, but entirely worth the effort. How can you put a price on seeing old friends, perhaps for the last time? And it was certainly worth coming here to see you. I hadn't counted on that."

Tears blurred Cara's vision. "No, I hadn't counted on seeing you again either. I'm so glad I came."

One of their friends stood and raised his glass. "To Mitzi, the Queen Bee of our little circle of old friends. Long may she reign."

"To Mitzi."

After the toast, the table went very quiet, as each person wrestled with their own thoughts about the impending loss of their old friend. It was all Cara could do not to curl into a ball and weep.

"All right, you bunch," Mitzi said, emphatically setting down her glass. "Save the eulogies for the funeral. Let's have some fun tonight. I want to dance."

Martin pushed her out onto the dance floor and whirled her around in time to the music. Cara watched them with a smile on her face. Their courage awed her. They'd decided that, in whatever time they were given, they would love one another. Because even though they knew their parting would be painful, they also believed that their love was worth the pain.

Love was worth the risk.

"Cara."

She looked up at the familiar voice. Peter stood beside her chair, his arm around a beautiful young blonde woman. Cara slowly got to her feet, her heart pumping double time. Seeing him again was the moment she'd both dreaded and looked forward to for the past six weeks. She managed a smile. "Peter. I heard you were coming to the reunion."

"Yes, Jenna told me you were planning to attend. Cara, this is my friend Samantha. Samantha, my ex-wife, Cara, my children's mother."

Cara extended her hand. "Hello."

"Hello."

She tried to decide whether Samantha felt any emotion at all in meeting her—jealousy, rivalry, hatred—but the only emotion she could detect was indifference.

"Sam, why don't you get yourself a drink at the bar?" He reached into his pocket and pulled out a few bills. "I need to talk to Cara about the girls for a few moments."

Samantha plucked the money out of Peter's hand and turned away without a word. Peter sighed as he watched her go. "She's bored."

"Then why did you bring her? You knew she wouldn't know anyone here."

He shrugged, and one side of his mouth went up in the grin she used to find so appealing. "She's a good-looking woman. What other reason do I need?"

For a moment, Cara actually felt sorry for the girl. She was nothing but arm candy to Peter. She looked at her ex-husband more closely. What had happened to the deep vertical lines between his brows? Was his hair less gray than the last time she'd seen him? She sighed. It wasn't her concern how Peter treated his girlfriend, or whether he used Botox and hair dye to make himself feel younger.

"You wanted to talk about the girls?"

He pulled her a little farther away from Mitzi and Martin's table. "They're scheduled to stay with me the last two weeks in July, but something's come up. We'll have to do it another time."

Anger rose inside Cara's chest and she struggled to keep it under control. "What's more important than spending time with your daughters? They've been looking forward to having you all to themselves at the lake for a long time."

"I told you, something's come up. Just tell them I'll make it up to them later."

"Oh no, no way. I'm not doing your dirty work for

you. If you're going to cancel, you're going to tell them yourself, and you'd better have a damn good reason."

Peter pursed his lips, clearly annoyed. "For cripes sake, Cara, do you have to make a federal case out of this? I said I'd do something with the girls another time."

"Exactly when will you pencil family time into your busy schedule?"

"Listen, I send plenty of money for the girls. I give them everything they need."

"Everything but your time. Believe it or not, sometimes money isn't enough. What can possibly take priority over your children?"

He took a swallow of his drink, glancing over to the bar where Samantha sipped a martini. "Sam and her friends have rented a cabin in the Adirondacks. She wants me to come."

Cara stared at him in disbelief. "You're blowing off the girls to spend two weeks with a bunch of twenty-year-olds?"

"Look, Sam wants me to come, and if I don't, she'll hook up with someone else."

She wondered if he knew how sad that sounded. His relationship with his girlfriend was so tenuous that his absence for even a short time could mean the end of it. "Are you sure she's worth the trouble?"

He grinned. "She's definitely worth the trouble. The sex is fantastic, and it doesn't hurt the ego to have a beautiful young woman on my arm. I can tell you, plenty of guys my age are envious."

A light flashed on in Cara's head. Suddenly, it was all so clear. "Is this what everything is about? The divorce, the heartache for me and the girls, the feeling that none of us is good enough for you? It's about making guys your age jealous because you've got a hot young girlfriend?"

Peter's smile disappeared "I woke up one morning and realized I was forty years old. My life was half over and I hadn't done any of the things I wanted to do when I was twenty. I hadn't traveled, I hadn't seen the world. And the only woman I'd ever slept with was you. I wanted to experience life, meet interesting people, do interesting things. I wanted a life!"

"I guess you got what you wanted. Has it been worth it?"

He glanced toward Samantha again. "For the most part. It hasn't been easy keeping up with Sam and her friends, but I've managed. It keeps me in shape." He laughed and rubbed his flat belly. "Not bad for a forty-three-year-old, is it?"

She cocked her head and took a good look at the man who had been her husband, her lover, for twenty years. Had she really ever known him?

"Are you happy, Peter?"

"Happy?" He repeated the word as if he'd never heard it before. "Sure, I guess I'm happy. Whatever that means."

She suddenly felt overwhelming pity for him. He was so insecure about his age that he'd willingly jettisoned his family for a never-ending pursuit of the fountain of youth. When had he become so shallow that appearances meant everything? Nothing seemed to matter more than having an attractive young girlfriend, a face free of lines, and hair without a trace of gray.

And then she was angry, with Peter and with herself. For three years she'd been certain the divorce had been her fault, that she'd been lacking because he didn't want her anymore, when all along his midlife crisis and his selfishness had been to blame. She'd wasted three years beating herself up and being afraid to love again.

No more.

"I really feel sorry that you're losing touch with Jenna and Beth. They're beautiful, amazing young women. Someday you'll regret that you didn't take the time to get to know them." She leaned forward and kissed his cheek. "Peter, I'll always be grateful to you for giving me our daughters. Please phone them on Monday and break the news. Have a nice life."

She turned and walked back to the table where Mitzi and Martin and their friends were making more toasts. She raised her glass. "To reconnecting with old friends and making new ones. And to new beginnings."

"Hear, hear," Mitzi exclaimed. "I'm all for new beginnings."

Everyone raised a glass and toasted Cara. "To new beginnings."

Suddenly she couldn't wait to get home. She set her half empty wine glass on the table and bent to hug Mitzi. "Now that I've found you again, we have to keep in touch." She reached into her purse and found a notepad and a pen. She scribbled her contact info. "Here's my e-mail address and phone number. What's yours?"

Mitzi gave her the information and she wrote it down, stowing the notepad in her purse once more. "It was wonderful seeing you again."

Mitzi smiled. "You, too, Miss New York."

They both knew they'd likely never see each other

again. Cara kissed her cheek, fighting to keep the tears at bay.

"Be happy, Cara."

"I'm really going to try. That's why I need to hurry home."

"Oh, sounds very intriguing. Promise you'll write and tell all the juicy details?"

"I promise, Miss Brainiac."

She laughed, and Cara kissed her cheek once more, savoring the softness of her friend's skin and the fresh scent of Dove soap. She'd forever associate that scent with Mitzi. She hugged Martin and kissed his cheek. "Look after her," she whispered in his ear.

He kissed her back. "I will."

She shook hands with all the others around the table, wishing she'd taken the time to get to know these interesting people back in high school. But she couldn't look back. It was time to face her future. She just hoped her future still wanted her.

****

Finn stuck the spoon directly into the ice cream container, pulling out a heaping dollop of double chocolate chip. He stuck the whole thing in his mouth, waiting for the rush of pleasure that ice cream used to give him.

Nothing.

If it came to a choice between the rush of eating ice cream and the pleasure of holding Cara in his arms, fudge ripple didn't stand a chance.

Disgusted with himself for resorting to old bad habits, he pushed the ice cream container back into the freezer. What the hell was he doing? It was two in the morning and he was prowling his house like a cat burglar. *Get some sleep already, you idiot.*

Not that he'd slept much since Cara had given him the boot. He'd gone over and over their last night together, dissecting everything they'd said, everything they'd done, remembering the passion and the pain. Especially the passion.

How was he supposed to forget the way she'd touched him? How could he forget the taste of her kiss or the way she felt in his arms, the smell of her perfume? At what point would he stop missing the girls and worrying that they'd be angry at him for the way it ended? And when would he stop hoping that Cara would fall in love with him the way he'd fallen in love with her?

He flopped onto the couch and threw an arm over his eyes. If he could just turn off his brain for a few minutes, maybe he could sleep.

The doorbell rang, making him sit straight up, his brain on full alert. Who could be at his door at this time of the morning?

He used the peephole to see who was at the door. When he saw Cara on his front step, he blinked and stumbled back, thinking he'd totally lost his mind and had begun conjuring up her presence. This figment of his imagination was even wearing a very sexy black dress. But when the doorbell rang a second time, he looked through the peephole again and realized Cara truly was standing on his doorstep, in the flesh. He wrenched open the door.

"Hello, Finn. I know it's late, but I saw your lights on and I was hoping we could talk. May I come in?"

He stood aside to let her in, not trusting himself to speak. As she passed him, Finn caught the spicy-sweet scent of her perfume, and myriad memories tumbled through his brain. He closed the door, then cleared his throat. "I thought you were at your reunion tonight."

"I was, but I didn't stay long."

"How come?" She'd been preparing for weeks for this reunion. Why would she leave so abruptly?

He watched her throat work as she swallowed. She lifted her gaze to his. "Because I needed to see you."

Finn pushed down the elation that blossomed in his heart, knowing his hopes could easily be dashed in the next moment. A sudden thought had him stepping toward her. "The girls are okay?"

"They're fine—aside from missing you and being angry with me."

"Why are they angry at you?"

"For sending you away."

She began to pace his small living room. "I've been driving around your block for almost an hour, trying to get up the courage to come to the door. I wouldn't have blamed you if you'd told me to get lost and never come back."

Finn watched as she walked back and forth in front of his sofa, wringing her hands and twisting the straps of her purse. Her long, slender legs covered the distance in three strides before having to turn to repeat the journey. Agitation clearly showed on her beautiful face. He couldn't stand seeing her in such distress.

"Cara, stop." He caught her hand and made her sit on the sofa. "Can I get you a drink of water, or maybe some tea?"

"Oh, God!" She dissolved into tears. "You're being so nice to me, and I've been so horrible to you."

His heart broke. However awful he'd been feeling,

nothing was worse than seeing Cara cry. "Sweetheart, please don't cry." He awkwardly patted her back, afraid that if he held her she'd send him away again. "Tell me what's wrong. What's happened?"

She took a deep breath and pulled a tissue from her purse to blow her nose. "I wanted to tell you that you were right."

"About what?"

She dabbed at her eyes. "There is something special between us. And it's more than the sex, which is pretty fantastic, by the way."

He grinned. "It was, wasn't it?"

"What we have together is so much more. I used the difference in our ages as an excuse because I was too scared of being hurt again. But the age difference doesn't matter at all because of everything we share. I wouldn't let myself see that. Until tonight."

"What happened tonight?"

She smiled, her eyelashes starred to points by her tears. "I guess I learned a couple of lessons at the reunion about what love really looks like." She reached out and touched his hand. "I love you, Finn."

He couldn't believe he was hearing this. He'd prayed for it, hoped for it, but now that Cara was here on his sofa telling him she loved him, it was so much sweeter than he'd ever imagined.

"I love you too." He cupped her face, his thumb wiping away the last of her tears. "So, where do we go from here?"

She wound her arms around his neck. "I don't know about you, but the first place I'd like to go from here is upstairs to your bedroom." She didn't have to ask twice.

Epilogue

Houston, Texas, One Year Later

As per Mitzi's wishes, the group gathered in the spacious backyard of the house that Mitzi and Martin had shared for seventeen years. In one of the many e-mails she'd sent Cara after the reunion in Summerville, she'd told her she wanted her funeral to feel like a picnic with friends, a happy celebration of life rather than a time for tears and maudlin speeches.

Cara did her best not to disappoint her friend by breaking down like a blubbering idiot.

It helped that Finn stood next to her, a strong shoulder to lean on. She'd leaned on him a lot in the past year. He was always there for her, encouraging her through good times and bad. But mostly they'd been very good. She was happier than she could ever remember. Her daughters were doing well, and they both adored him. Her mother finally realized she meant business and had quit trying to contact her. Her job as host of *Rochester Noon* had its challenges, but most days she couldn't wait to get to work to discover what interesting person she'd meet that day.

Life was sweet. And precious. She only had to look around at the sad faces assembled in Martin's backyard to understand that.

One after another, Mitzi's friends stood and told

funny stories of their adventures with her over the years, her crazy quirks and foibles, and her incredible gift for making friends and keeping them. Many tears were shed but, just as Mitzi had wished, there was much laughter as well.

Then it was Cara's turn. She rose from her seat and faced the group. In the past year she'd gotten to know them all through e-mails and phone calls, and through Mitzi's stories. She'd been particularly determined that Cara get to know her friends and become part of the group she called the "Summerville Geeks." Mitzi teased her that in high school she would rather have stood naked on the fifty-yard line during halftime at the homecoming football game than be part of her group. Now, Cara was pleased to be considered an honorary Geek.

"This is exactly what Mitzi wanted. Good friends, good food, good wine. Wherever she is, I'm sure she's looking down on us and saying, "Get up and dance, people! And have another drink!""

Everyone laughed and nodded.

"I owe a lot to her. She showed me much friendship and love in the last year. Without her, I wouldn't have met all of you. And without her and Martin showing me the way, I wouldn't know what true love is." She smiled at Finn and reached for his hand. "I wouldn't have had the courage to tell Finn how much I loved him, and we wouldn't be having a baby in five months."

A hoot of surprise and joy went up from the group. Martin embraced her, and then kissed her cheek, tears in his eyes.

"Mitzi would be so pleased for you."

"I know. We've decided if it's a girl that we want to call her Mitzi."

Martin laughed. "Oh, God, don't do that! Mitzi hated her name. If it's a girl, call her Michelle. That's the name Mitzi wanted to name our daughter, if we'd had one."

Tears filled Cara's eyes as she turned to Finn. "What do you think of Michelle for a name?"

He tenderly brushed away her tears. "I think it's beautiful."

"I can hardly wait to see the new baby next year," Martin said. "The Geeks are meeting for the annual get-together at a resort in Vermont. You'll be there, won't you?"

She turned to her husband. More than anything she wanted to be part of this amazing, loving group of people. For too long her life had been ruled by appearances, and by concerns for what other people would think. If there was one thing she'd learned from Mitzi it was that the only thing that mattered was how happy something made her.

And she'd been right. Marrying Finn had made her very happy.

"What do you think?" she asked her husband.

He grinned. "I think we'll be there with bells on."

A word about the author...

Jana Richards has tried her hand at many writing projects over the years, from magazine articles and short stories to novellas and full-length novels. Since she's never met a romance genre she didn't like, her published works include an eclectic mix of romantic suspense, romantic comedy, contemporary romance, and historical romantic suspense. From time to time she enjoys throwing in a touch of the paranormal, just for fun. She has a soft spot for romantic comedy and loves to create characters with a sense of humor that (hopefully) makes them as much fun to read as they are to write.

When not writing up a storm, working at her day job as an Office Administrator or dealing with ever-present mountains of laundry, Jana can be found on the local golf course, pursuing her newest hobby.

Jana has two beautiful grownup daughters and lives in Western Canada with her husband and a highly spoiled Pug/Terrier cross named Lou.

You can reach Jana through her website at
www.janarichards.net

Thank you for purchasing
this Wild Rose Press publication.

For questions or more information
contact us at
info@thewildrosepress.com.

The Wild Rose Press
www.TheWildRosePress.com

To visit with authors of The Wild Rose Press join our
yahoo loop at
http://groups.yahoo.com/group/thewildrosepress/